...are out standing
in their field!

W9-CSN-769

#7 ATTACK OF THE
TWO-TON TOMATOES

#7 ATTACK OF THE
TWO-TON TOMATOES

MIKE FORD

Based upon the television series "Eerie Indiana"
created by Karl Schaefer and José Rivera

AN AVON CAMELOT BOOK

This is a work of fiction. Names, characters, places and incidents either are the product of the author's imagination or are used fictitiously. Any resemblance to actual events, locales, organizations, or persons, living or dead, is entirely coincidental and beyond the intent of either the author or the publisher.

AVON BOOKS
A division of
The Hearst Corporation
1350 Avenue of the Americas
New York, New York 10019

Copyright © 1998 by Hearst Entertainment, Inc.
Based on the Hearst Entertainment television series entitled ''Eerie Indiana'' created by Karl Schaefer and José Rivera
Published by arrangement with Hearst Entertainment, Inc.
Excerpt from *Goners #1: RU1:2* copyright © 1998 by Jamie S. Simons and E. W. Scollon, Jr.
Visit our website at **http://www.AvonBooks.com**
Library of Congress Catalog Card Number: 97-94042
ISBN: 0-380-79783-6

First Avon Camelot Printing: February 1998

CAMELOT TRADEMARK REG. U.S. PAT. OFF. AND IN OTHER COUNTRIES, MARCA REGISTRADA, HECHO EN U.S.A.

Printed in the U.S.A.

OPM   10   9   8   7   6   5   4   3   2   1

PROLOGUE

My name is Marshall Teller. Not too long ago, I was living in New Jersey, just across the river from New York City. It was crowded, polluted, and full of crime. I loved it. But my parents wanted a better life for my sister and me. So we moved to a place so wholesome, so squeaky clean, so ordinary that you could only find it on TV—Eerie, Indiana.

It's the American Dream come true, right? Wrong. Sure, my new home town *looks* normal enough. But look again. Underneath, it's crawling with strange stuff. Item: Elvis lives on my paper route. Item: Bigfoot eats out of my trash. Item: I see unexplained flashing lights in the sky at least once a week. No one believes me, but Eerie is the center of weirdness for the entire planet.

Since I moved here, I've had my brain sucked out and put back in, relived the same day over and over thanks to a cursed snow globe, and been stalked by a grudge-bearing tornado named Bob. Every time something strange happens, I think my life can't get any more peculiar. But then I turn a corner and there's something even stranger waiting for me. But no matter how weird Eerie gets, nobody else seems to notice.

Nobody except my friend Simon Holmes. Simon's my next-door neighbor. He's lived in Eerie his whole life, and he's the only other person who knows just how freaky this place is. Together, we've been keeping a record of all the stuff that happens around here. We've faced some of Eerie's most bizarre inhabitants and lived to tell about it, from the talking dogs that tried to take over the city to the crazy woman who kidnapped us and tried to keep us locked up forever in giant plastic kitchenware. I told you this place was weird.

Still don't believe me? You will.

1

When my dad came home from work that Tuesday night a few weeks ago, I had no idea that it was the beginning of another adventure into the weirdness that is Eerie, Indiana. I just thought he was in a really good mood.

"Hey!" he yelled as he came in the door and tossed his briefcase onto the floor. "Guess what happened to me today?"

He came into the kitchen with a big smile on his face. I was sitting at the table figuring out which of my customers on my paper route had paid me and which ones hadn't. My mom was going through the refrigerator in her once-every-six-months cleaning frenzy, tossing out all of the leftovers that were sprouting unidentifiable molds.

"Where's Syndi?" Dad asked.

"Where else?" I answered. "On the phone."

"Syndi," Dad yelled up the stairs. "Hang up and come down here. I have an announcement to make."

It wasn't like my dad to have surprises. I looked over at my mom, but she just shrugged and threw a piece of what looked like cheese covered with fuzzy blue fur into the bulging trash bag at her feet.

"What's the big news?" I asked my dad.

"Wait until your sister is here," he said. "This is really exciting. I don't want her to miss it."

I tried to think of what could possibly be so thrilling that it would make my dad call a family meeting. I mean, the most exciting thing he usually has to tell us is that he had lunch at Eerie Chicken, or that we're going to Great Aunt Ingrid's house to see another one of her weird home movies. This had to be something major.

Syndi came into the kitchen and sat down at the table. "I hope this is good," she said. "Patsy was just telling me about how she and Edina went to the mall and found the cutest dresses for the dance this weekend."

"How could you tear yourself away?" I said, teasing her.

"Okay, okay," my dad said. "Just let me talk."

He looked at all three of us in turn. We were all staring at him, waiting anxiously. He cleared his throat.

"I have something to tell you," he said. "Something that is going to affect all of us. Now, this might seem like a big change, but . . ."

"Are we moving?" I yelled. "Are we leaving Eerie and going back to New Jersey?" I couldn't think of anything else that would be a bigger change in our lives, and I hoped it was true.

4

"No, Mars," my dad said. "We aren't moving."

"Are we getting a new car?" shrieked Syndi, suddenly excited. "Oh, Daddy, can I have the old one? Please? You know I'm just about to get my license, and . . ."

"No!" my dad said again. He sounded annoyed. "We are not getting a new car. And even if we were, you are far too young to . . ."

"I know," my mom interrupted. "We're going to the Petrified Forest for vacation. Oh, Edgar, I knew you'd agree that Hawaii would be boring."

"We are *not* going anywhere on vacation," my dad said firmly. "We are *not* moving, and we are *not* getting a new car. Now, would you all please just be quiet so I can finish what I have to say?"

We all looked at him, not saying a word. After a minute, when he was sure we weren't going to interrupt him, he started to speak again.

"Now, as I was saying, I have an announcement to make. It's something very, very exciting."

He paused, and we all leaned forward. I was about to burst from the anticipation, and I could tell that Syndi and my mom were, too.

"You are looking," he said, "at the new assistant head of testing for the most important project that Things has ever undertaken."

Things, Incorporated, is the company my dad works for. It's why we moved to Eerie in the first place. See, statistically speaking, Eerie is the most normal place in

5

the United States. If you average everyone in Eerie to-gether, each family has exactly 2.3 kids, 1.2 cars, and 2.1 pets. Perfectly normal in every way. The theory is that if a product like sneakers or shampoo or TV dinners is popular in Eerie, then it will be popular all over the country. So companies hire Things, Inc., to test out new products for them. That's what my dad does.

Since we'd moved to Eerie, I'd learned that statistics lie—big time. But my dad loved his job at Things, Inc., and he worked hard. Now it seemed he was moving up the corporate ladder. Still, his announcement wasn't what I'd been expecting. Mom, Syndi, and I all ex-changed glances. After everything that we thought Dad might be going to say, this was sort of a letdown.

"That's great, honey," my mom said finally, in a voice that I could tell meant she was still thinking about the Petrified Forest.

"Yeah," said Syndi. "This is much cooler than get-ting a new car. Way cooler." She didn't sound very convincing.

"So, um, what's the project?" I asked.

"That's the best part," he said. "We all get to be involved."

He disappeared into the living room. When he came back, he was carrying a big paper grocery bag, which he set on the table.

"What's in there?" I asked. I knew enough to be suspicious about some of the stuff that Things, Inc. tested.

"Wait until you see this," he said. He reached into the bag and pulled out something that looked like a shiny red softball.

"What on earth is that?" my mother said.

"That," said my father, "is what is going to make Edgar Teller the most important person at Things, Inc."

"But what *is* it?" said Syndi.

"It's a tomato," my dad said proudly.

"A tomato?" I said. "No tomato is that big."

"That's what's so great about it," he said. "This is the latest in designer vegetables. And the best part is, they're grown right here in Eerie by our very own Eerie Farms."

"You're working on giant tomatoes?" my mom said skeptically.

"Not just tomatoes," said my dad. He reached into the bag and pulled out some more items. "There are peas, beans, radishes, and broccoli. And that's just the beginning. If these take off, there's going to be a whole line of Eerie Farms produce. And you're looking at the man who's going to be responsible for test-marketing them."

We all sat staring at the vegetables on the table in front of us. The pea pods were at least a foot long. When my mother picked one up and opened it, peas the size of golf balls rolled out. The broccoli looked like a small forest of oddly shaped trees. The beans were as big around as my thumb.

"How do they get them so big?" I asked.

"I don't know exactly," said my dad. "My job is just to see if people like them."

"And do they?" asked my mother doubtfully.

"That's what we're going to find out right now," he said. "We're going to be the very first family in all of Eerie to try them."

"Wonderful," said my mother, holding up a bean.

"Swell," said Syndi, eyeing the peas.

"I can't wait," I said, trying to break off a broccoli stalk.

Half an hour later, the stove was covered with steaming pots of water. My father had put on the apron he wears when he's barbecuing, and he was standing in front of the pots, putting the giant vegetables into them and watching them cook. As he did, he was making notes in a little notebook.

"Just look at those peas," he said, writing something down. "What a bright green. They look so fresh."

He lifted another lid. "Wow," he exclaimed, "that broccoli smells fantastic."

When the vegetables were finished cooking, he put them into bowls and set them on the table. Then he took the colossal tomato and cut it into pieces as big as slices of toast.

"Okay," he said. "Let's eat."

I sat down and looked at the bowls of vegetables. They looked so weird that I really didn't want to try them. But my dad was so excited about them, and about his promotion, that I couldn't let him down. Reluctantly,

I spooned a few of the big peas onto my plate. Spearing one with my fork, I crammed it into my mouth and started to chew.

"Hey," I said after a few bites, "this is really good."

And it *was* good. Usually I can take or leave vegetables. You know, they aren't the most disgusting things in the whole world, but they certainly aren't my favorites, either. On the whole, I'd be happier with a hot dog than a lima bean.

But there was something about those peas. Something different. It wasn't that they tasted any less pealike or anything, they just tasted—well—better than regular peas. Fresher. Sweeter. More delicious. I found myself wanting to eat another one, and then another. Before I knew it, I'd eaten a whole plate of them.

After the peas, I tried a slice of the tomato. It was so big that I had to cut it into smaller chunks, and each mouthful was like eating a little piece of summer. The juice filled my mouth and made me think of long hot days with nothing to do. It was just amazing. I'd never tasted anything so good before.

My mom and Syndi seemed to be enjoying the vegetables just as much as I was. Syndi had eaten almost half of the broccoli, and I had to grab some before she wolfed it all down. My mother was busily snapping the beans in half and devouring them one after the next. She'd already made short work of the radishes.

"These are just wonderful," Syndi said. "I could eat this broccoli all day. What do they do to it to make it taste so good?"

"It's all scientific," my father said. "I don't really understand all of it. Mr. Plante said it has something to do with altering the DNA in the vegetables so they have only the best qualities."

Mr. Plante was my dad's boss at Things, Inc. He'd been hired by the company a few months before, and the first thing he did was make my dad his special assistant. Dad was really excited when it happened, because it meant someone was noticing all the good work he'd been doing.

"And you said they're grown here in Eerie?" I asked.

"That's right," he said. "Out at Eerie Farms. They've been working on these for quite a while, and now it's time to test-market them to see if people like them."

"Well, if they all taste like these do," I said, "people are going to *love* them."

"That's exactly what we're hoping for," my dad said. "We want Eerie Farms produce to be on every table in America. We're going to be the company that actually gets kids all across the country to like vegetables. It will be the best thing since . . . well since . . ."

"Since chocolate-flavored breakfast cereal," I said.

"Since instant pizza," added Syndi.

"Since Foreverware," my mom exclaimed.

I didn't agree with my mom about that one, but I had to agree that the vegetables from Eerie Farms were something else. In fact, they were so good that I completely forgot that they were grown in Eerie, and that anything that came from our town couldn't be one hundred percent normal.

For the next hour or so, my dad asked us a bunch of questions about the vegetables. Our answers were supposed to help the people at Things, Inc. figure out the best way to market the produce to the rest of the country. So while we talked, Dad wrote down how we felt about the vegetables' color, taste, texture, size, smell, and freshness. He asked us to rate each vegetable on a scale of one to ten. I gave the peas a ten and the tomatoes a nine, but just because I thought there might be a few too many seeds in them. The beans, radishes, and broccoli all got tens from Mom and Syndi.

Dad seemed really pleased with our responses to the questions. As he wrote, he kept smiling and nodding, and when he was done he shut his notebook with a satisfied snap.

"Well," he said. "I think Mr. Plante will be more than pleased with the results of our first taste test. How does it feel to be the first family in Eerie to enjoy Eerie Farms produce?"

"Great," I said. "So when will it be available in stores?"

"We're going to start testing it in Eerie first thing tomorrow," he said. "Some of the stores will sell it, and we're giving some to the restaurants. We're even trying it out at your school, Mars. If it does as well as we expect it to, then we'll start sending it to markets all over the country."

I was really proud of my dad. He was going to be involved in the biggest thing to hit the food market in years. As I helped him clean up the dishes, I tried to imagine what might be next for him at Things, Inc. Maybe, I thought, he could even become a vice president. All because of some really big tomatoes.

That night I had a strange dream. I was standing in a field. All around me there were little plants, like baby peas or something. I bent down to pick a pea pod. Then, all of a sudden, these tendrils shot out from the plants and began to wrap around my arms and legs. I struggled, but I couldn't get away. As I screamed for help, the plants wrapped me up in a cocoon of leaves and shoots, until finally even my mouth was covered and no one could hear me. That was creepy enough. But the weirdest thing was, I was sure that the whole time I was trying to get free I could hear someone laughing at me. And although I couldn't see anyone, I knew somehow that it was the plants that were laughing.

I woke up with a start and looked around my room. Everything was fine. It was morning. The sun was shining in the window and the birds were singing outside. There was nothing wrong. Relieved, I pulled the sheets back and got out of bed. I went into the bathroom and started to get into the shower.

Then I noticed something on my arm. On the underside of my forearm, just above my elbow, I had a little bit of a rash. The skin was sort of itchy, and it was discolored. Only instead of being red, like a normal rash should be, this one was green.

2

I scratched at the rash on my arm. It wasn't that itchy, and there weren't any bumps on the skin or anything. I had poison ivy once, the time Simon and I camped out in the Eerie Woods, and that rash had been horrible. I had big red blotches all over my body for weeks, and I had to cover myself with this pink lotion to make them stop itching. I thought I'd go crazy.

But this was different. It didn't hurt at all. In fact, where my skin had turned sort of greenish, it felt smooth, almost fuzzy. And the spot was only the size of a dime.

To tell the truth, I didn't really think much about it at all. I figured it was some sort of reaction to something I'd touched or gotten on my skin, and would just go away on its own. Besides, I was more concerned about the math test I had that morning. Because of our vegetable feast the night before, I hadn't done much studying for it, and I had to try to cram everything I could learn about geometry into my head before third period came around.

Grabbing my books from my desk, I ran downstairs and into the kitchen. My dad was pulling frozen waffles out of the toaster, and my mother was buttering a piece of toast. Syndi was nowhere to be seen, so I figured that she'd already left for school.

"Morning, Marshall," said my dad. "Want a waffle?"

"No time," I said, taking a quick drink of orange juice from the container. "I have a test this morning. I want to get to school and study a little."

"At least have some carrot sticks," my mom said, handing me a bag of them. "They're from the vegetables your dad brought home. They're really tasty. Maybe all the vitamins will help you be smarter for your test."

"Speaking of school," my dad said, "I believe we're going to start testing the Eerie Farms produce in your cafeteria today. We need to have untainted results, so don't talk to anyone about it, okay?"

"Sure thing, Dad," I said, running out the door. "Not a word."

As usual, Simon was waiting for me on the sidewalk outside his house. As we walked toward B. F. Skinner Junior High, he told me about the cool sci-fi movie he'd watched the night before. I got so wrapped up in his description of the plot—something about aliens invading the world by taking over the bodies of United States politicians—that I totally forgot about the giant vegetables we'd had for dinner the night before. And I certainly wasn't thinking about the rash on my arm.

"And at the end, the alien senators vote to turn all the humans over for experiments," said Simon as we went up the stairs to school. "Only no one suspects anything because they think they're just lowering taxes, and they can't believe that the people they voted for could be from Jupiter. It's so cool."

"It sounds great," I said. "You can tell me more at lunch. Right now I have to go study for this killer test."

Simon went off to his class, and I went to the library to study for a while. I concentrated on the formulas for figuring out the area of a square and the cubic feet in a cylinder. As I studied, I chomped on the bag of carrot sticks my mom had given me. Before long, my mind was racing with numbers, and when the bell finally rang, startling me back to my senses, I was surprised to see that I'd studied right through second period and it was time for my test. I reached for my books, and as I did I saw that the green rash on my arm had spread. It was now almost the size of a quarter.

I didn't have time to think about it, though. I had to get to class. I gathered up my stuff, crammed it into my backpack, and ran to class. As soon as everyone was seated, Mr. Pythagoras handed around the test papers and we got started. I chewed on the end of my pencil, trying to remember everything I'd studied just a few minutes ago about the lengths of the sides of a triangle and how to figure out the volume of a sphere.

As I got to work on the first problem, I realized that I was suddenly kind of thirsty, and I wished I'd gotten a drink before coming to class.

Forty minutes later, the bell rang again.

"Okay, everyone," said Mr. Pythagoras. "Pencils down. Drop your papers on my desk on the way out."

I scribbled down the last answer—or at least what I thought the answer was—and got up to go. It was lunch period, and I couldn't wait to get to the cafeteria. I was really thirsty now.

Simon was already in line when I reached the cafeteria, so he let me cut in with him.

"What's on the menu today?" I asked. Simon always knows what's for lunch. I've never seen a kid who is so into food.

"It should be pizza," he said. "Hopefully with pepperoni. I'm so hungry I could eat a horse."

"Well, in this place that might be exactly what you *are* eating," I joked.

The line inched forward, and we came to the food trays. Steam was rising up from them, and something smelled really good. But it wasn't pizza.

"Hey," said Simon when he got close enough to see what was being served. "What gives?"

Sitting in the steaming trays were piles of vegetables. Each tray held a different kind. Then I remembered what my dad had said about the Eerie Farms produce being tested at school.

"Who wants vegetables for lunch? And why are they

so funny looking?'' Simon said, staring at the large vegetables.

''It's what they gave us,'' said the sullen lunch lady behind the counter. The hair net holding her hair back was so tight it stretched the skin of her face so that her eyes were little slits. ''If you don't want it, don't eat it.''

''There's nothing else,'' said Simon. ''I guess I'll take it.''

''Corn or peas?'' said the lunch lady.

''Peas, I guess,'' said Simon unhappily.

The lunch lady scooped up a big pile of peas and slopped them into a bowl. She handed it to Simon, who looked at it and groaned.

''What do you want?'' the lunch lady asked me.

Remembering how good the vegetables had tasted the night before, I said, ''A little of both, please.''

The lunch lady cocked one eyebrow. ''A kid who likes vegetables. That's a first,'' she snorted as she handed me a plate.

Simon and I took our lunches to a table in the corner and sat down. I'd gotten a big glass of water, and as soon as I was seated I gulped down the whole thing.

''What are you, a camel?'' teased Simon.

''I've been really thirsty all morning,'' I said. ''I don't know why.''

Simon was poking at the peas on his plate. He had a disgusted look on his face. ''I can't believe they didn't have pizza,'' he said.

I took a bite of my corn. It was excellent—buttery and sweet and salty all at the same time.

"Just try it," I said. "You might be surprised."

Simon speared a pea with his fork and held it up.

"It's so big," he said. "It looks like a green Ping-Pong ball."

He opened his mouth and stuffed the pea inside. As he started chewing it, I watched the expression on his face change from one of repulsion to one of delight. He chewed faster, then swallowed.

"Wow," he said. "That was the most amazing pea I've ever had."

He ate another pea, and then another one. Pretty soon he was shoveling peas into his mouth as quickly as he could swallow them.

"These are really good," he said when he'd eaten almost the whole bowl.

I nodded. "I know," I said. Then I told him the story of how my dad was working on the Eerie Farms project. "But you can't tell anyone," I said. "They need the test results to be reliable."

"Don't worry about me," said Simon. "I may like these, but I'll never admit to anyone that I actually enjoy eating vegetables. It would ruin my reputation."

I looked around the cafeteria. At every table, kids were eating the vegetables like they were chocolate pudding. It was an amazing sight. Usually the cafeteria is filled with the sounds of people talking and laughing. But that day it was silent except for the sounds of mouths chewing.

"I don't know what they do to this stuff," said Simon, "but whatever it is, it's working."

"It's weird, isn't it?" I said.

"What's that on your arm?" Simon asked.

I looked down. While we'd been talking, I had been absent-mindedly scratching the rash on my skin. Now I saw that the green spot was even bigger.

"I don't know what it is," I said. "It just sort of showed up this morning."

"Maybe you're allergic to something," Simon suggested. "I get spots all over if I eat walnuts."

"Yeah, but green ones?" I said.

"You never know," said Simon. "Have you been eating anything unusual lately?"

I thought for a minute. "Just those vegetables," I said.

Simon laughed. "Just what every kid wishes for," he said, "to be allergic to vegetables."

I laughed, too. "Wouldn't that be funny? Finally, I'd have an excuse not to eat brussels sprouts."

"Well, it will probably go away in a day or two," said Simon. "I wouldn't worry about it."

And I didn't worry about it. At least not for a while. Over the next week, the rash didn't go away, but it didn't get much bigger, either. When Simon found a similar spot on his leg, we just assumed we'd both eaten something we were allergic to. It seemed odd that we would both get it, but by then we were used to weird things happening in Eerie.

During that week, it seemed like you couldn't go anywhere in Eerie without seeing the Eerie Farms vegetables or the new signs featuring their slogan: EERIE FARMS PRODUCE—SO GOOD, IT'S UNNATURAL! The vegetables had really caught on, and everyone wanted to try them. The supermarket had to build new cases just to hold the giant cauliflower, squashes, eggplant, and heads of lettuce that were unloaded daily and gone within a few hours as shoppers rushed to buy them. My dad said he'd never seen anything like it in all the years he'd been doing product testing.

"This is just phenomenal," he said one night at dinner as we tried the new Eerie Farms sweet potatoes. "People can't get enough of these vegetables. The demand is almost twice the supply. We're getting approval numbers like you've never seen. Why, this is going to change the way the whole country thinks about veggies."

Dad was particularly excited because his boss, Mr. Plante, kept telling him what a good job he was doing. We were seeing less and less of him as he spent longer hours at the office, planning new tests for the Eerie Farms produce and trying to think of different ways to market it.

I was really happy for my dad. But at the same time, I was starting to wonder a little bit about the Eerie Farms vegetables. They tasted great, but there was something just a little bit strange about how everyone was going crazy for them. Even my mom—who doesn't like to cook—was inventing new recipes, just so she could use the vegetables. She'd even gone out and bought a cookbook, *One Thousand and One Vegetarian Nights*. Every day when I came home from school, she was in the kitchen peeling, dicing, slicing, and chopping, trying out some strange new dish.

"Aren't you getting a little tired of vegetables?" I asked one night while we all sat at the table eating an asparagus and rutabaga soufflé my mother had whipped up.

Mom, Dad, and Syndi all laughed, as though I'd just said the funniest thing any of them had ever heard.

"Tired of vegetables?" said Syndi. "Are you crazy? I could eat these all the time."

"Well, we have been," I said. "We had broccoli pancakes for breakfast, steamed carrots for lunch, and now this. All I've eaten for a week now has come from Eerie Farms."

"I know," said my dad. "Isn't that great? I'm telling you, this stuff is going to put Eerie on the map."

I pushed a pile of soufflé around my plate. I didn't want to ruin my dad's excitement, but for some reason I didn't really feel like eating.

"Do you know exactly how they're growing the vegetables?" I asked my father. "You know, how they're getting them so big."

"I haven't really thought about it, Marshall," he said. "I've been too busy working on the tests to think about anything else."

"I was just wondering," I said.

My dad put his fork down. "I'll tell you what," he

said. "Why don't you and I take a little trip out to Eerie Farms this weekend? We can see the whole operation."

"Really?" I said.

He nodded. "Sure," he said. "It would probably be good for me to see it, anyway. You can even bring Simon along."

"Thanks, Dad," I said. "That would be really great."

Suddenly, I felt a little better. I even felt a little silly for worrying about the vegetables. After all, I thought, how can vegetables possibly be bad for you?

I was about to find out.

3

On Saturday morning, Simon and I piled into the back of my dad's car for the ride out to Eerie Farms. We were both excited about seeing how the vegetables were grown, and Simon had even brought along a notebook to write down everything we found out.

"This is going to be so cool," he said as we drove through town and onto Route 13. "We'll be the first ones to get a look at the Eerie Farms operation."

"I understand it's very impressive," said my father. "You boys are lucky—very few people have been to the fields. They're keeping their secrets very hush-hush."

After about twenty minutes, we turned off of Route 13 and onto the dirt road that led to Eerie Farms. I was surprised to see a sign that said PRIVATE PROPERTY: KEEP OFF! posted on the side of the road.

"Wow, they really want to keep people out, don't they?" I said.

"It's just a precaution," my father replied. "They don't want anyone trying to steal their secrets."

The more we drove, the more signs we saw. Some of them looked like the first one. Others said things like STAY OUT or AUTHORIZED PERSONNEL ONLY.

"This is starting to look like some kind of military base or something," I said, but my dad just chuckled.

Finally we turned a curve in the road and came to a big gate. Two men stood in front of it. They were dressed in green uniforms and wore sunglasses. One of the men held up his hand for us to stop, and we came to a halt. The man walked over to the car.

"Do you have any identification?" he asked.

"I'm Edgar Teller," my dad said, showing the man his ID card. "From Things, Incorporated. This is my son, Marshall, and his friend Simon."

The man looked at each of us. He was frowning.

"Is this visit authorized?" he asked.

"I'm working on the Eerie Farms produce project," my dad said. "I work with Mr. Plante."

"Oh, with Mr. Plante," said the man, as though my dad had just announced that he worked for the White House or something. "In that case, come right in."

He went to the gate and unlocked it, swinging it open so that we could drive through. As soon as we had passed, he shut it again, and the two men took their places blocking the road.

"He sure seemed to be impressed when you mentioned Mr. Plante," I said to my dad. "He must be pretty important around here."

"Well, he *is* in charge of the test marketing," said my dad. "I guess that counts for something."

We drove up the road some more until we came to wide fields filled with growing plants. On either side of us, men were working in the fields. They were all wearing the same green uniforms the guards had been wearing. On the backs, the words EERIE FARMS were printed in yellow, and there was a picture of a big red tomato.

We passed through the fields and came to a big barn. My dad stopped the car, and we got out. A man came walking out of the barn and waved to my dad.

"Hey there, Edgar," he said, shaking my dad's hand.

"Hi, Bud," my dad said.

He turned to Simon and me. "Boys, this is Bud. He runs things around here."

"Hi," I said. "I'm Marshall, and this is my friend Simon."

Bud shook our hands. "It's good to meet you," he said. "Your dad tells me you're interested in how we do things out here at Eerie Farms."

"We're sort of curious," I said. "We were just wondering how it is you get the vegetables so big."

"And tasty," added Simon.

Bud laughed. He seemed so nice that I was almost embarrassed that I'd thought the produce from Eerie Farms was strange in any way.

"Why don't I give you the guided tour?" he said. "I can't tell you all our secrets, of course, but I can show you some things I think you'll find very interesting."

We started to walk toward the barn, but then Bud stopped. He pulled something out of his back pocket.

"Almost forgot," he said, handing Simon and I each a baseball cap decorated with the farm logo. "Can't let you go running around without an Eerie Farms hat now, can I?"

Simon and I put the caps on. "Thanks," I said. I know it sounds silly, but I felt really cool in the hat, like I was part of the team or something.

We followed Bud as he walked behind the barn. There we saw three big glass buildings.

"These are our greenhouses," Bud said, opening the door to the first building and motioning for us to step inside.

Inside the greenhouse, the air was hot and steamy. The room was filled with tables covered with trays of seedlings, and a constant mist fell on the plants from hoses overhead. I felt as though we were standing in the middle of a tropical rain forest.

"This is where it all starts," explained Bud. "Before any of our vegetables make it to the fields, we try them out here in the greenhouse."

"What are these?" I asked, examining the trays of plants.

"These are a new kind of cucumber we're working on," he said. "Would you believe we just planted them this morning?"

"This morning?" I said. "But they're already almost six inches tall."

Bud grinned. "We've learned how to make quick-growing vegetables," he said. "That's one of the reasons our produce tastes so fresh. It grows from seed to plants in just about a day, so when you get it from the store, it's almost like picking it right off the vine.''

I watched the cucumber plants, and in only a few minutes they formed vines and then flowers where the cucumbers would be. It was like watching a movie on fast forward.

"This is incredible," I said. "How do you do that?"

Bud pointed to the hoses overhead. "We've developed a very special kind of plant food," he said. "We mix it into the water and give the seedlings a continuous spray of it. That gives them a head start."

"What's in the plant food?" asked Simon.

"I don't really know," Bud said. "In order to keep the recipe top secret, I only know one of the ingredients. Other people also know one ingredient. When it comes time to make more fertilizer, we each add our ingredient to the tank, but we never know exactly what the others are adding. That way no one can steal the secret formula."

"What a good idea," I said. I was still watching the cucumber vines, which continued to grow while Bud was talking. Now tiny cucumbers replaced the blossoms, and they were growing so quickly they looked like balloons filling up with water.

"Want to see the next step?" asked Bud.

"You mean there's more?" I said incredulously. After what I'd been watching, I couldn't imagine it got any better.

"Oh, yes," said Bud. "You've only seen part of the farm."

We left the greenhouse and walked over to a nearby field. A group of men wearing the green Eerie Farms uniforms were working on something, but I couldn't see what it was. Then, as we got closer, I realized that they were all standing around a pumpkin.

"What are they doing to it?" asked Simon.

"They're trying out our new growth formula fertilizer," said Bud. "It's the latest step forward in the technology we use to make our vegetables bigger than regular ones."

As we looked on, one of the men went over to the pumpkin and sprayed it with what looked like a squirt bottle filled with water. Then everyone stood back and watched. At first, nothing happened. Then, after a minute or two, the pumpkin began to swell. The sides began to pump in and out, and the stem started to get longer and thicker.

After another minute, the pumpkin started to blow up very quickly. First it was the size of a basketball, then it was the size of a small dog. It kept growing, getting bigger and bigger, until it was bigger than a bicycle.

"Is it going to stop?" I whispered to Bud.

"We'll see," he said mysteriously. He was watching the pumpkin intently, and his eyes were sparkling.

The pumpkin continued to grow until it was the size of a small car. I couldn't even believe my eyes. I was sure it had to be a trick. I looked over at Simon and saw that his mouth was hanging open in shock.

Finally, the pumpkin stopped growing. It gave one final twitch and was still. When the men were sure it wasn't going to grow any larger, they all ran over and started taking measurements and doing tests on it.

"What did you think of that?" Bud asked us.

I couldn't speak. Neither could Simon. We just stood there, staring at each other and trying to think of something to say.

"That was . . ." I started.

"Really cool," finished Simon.

I nodded in agreement. There really wasn't anything else to say to describe what we'd just witnessed.

"That's just one of the new things we're working on," said Bud. "We intend to make Eerie Farms produce the most talked-about vegetables in the world."

"Well, if you can get them all to do what that pumpkin did, then you won't have any problems doing that," I said. "You could feed all of Indiana on that one pumpkin."

"So, do you boys feel better about eating the stuff from Eerie Farms?" my dad asked.

"I sure do," said Simon.

"Yeah," I said. "I guess I do, too. It really is all just science, isn't it?"

"Did you boys have some worries?" Bud asked.

"Well, you can never be too sure," I said. I couldn't believe I'd even thought that something weird was going on.

Bud looked at me, and for a second it seemed like

his smile disappeared. Then it was back again, and he was his usual jolly self.

"Why don't we go have some lunch?" he said. "You can try our new beets. Just grew 'em yesterday. You can be our first test audience."

"Great," I said. "After seeing all of these plants, I'm starving."

"Me, too," said Simon.

"Okay, then," said Bud. "Let's head over to the cafeteria."

We were almost to the building where the cafeteria was when I realized that I'd dropped my hat back by the giant pumpkin. In all the excitement, I hadn't even realized it was gone.

"I'll be right back," I said as the others went inside to eat. "I'm just going to pick up my hat."

I ran back the way we'd come. When I got to the spot where the pumpkin was, the men were loading it onto a truck. They had tied a rope to the stalk, and they were trying to pull it up a ramp they'd made from some boards. They'd gotten it about halfway up the ramp, and they were trying to push and pull it the rest of the way.

"Be careful," one of the men was saying to another one, who was pushing the pumpkin from behind. "You don't want to break the skin and get any of that juice on your skin. Remember what happened to Jake."

What, I wondered, was wrong with getting the pumpkin juice on your skin? And who was Jake?

I found my hat where I'd dropped it on the ground

and I picked it up. I put it on and started to walk back toward the cafeteria. The men were still trying to load the pumpkin onto the truck. They were grunting and groaning as they strained to push the big vegetable up the ramp.

All of a sudden, someone yelled. I turned around and saw that one of the men had pushed too hard and his hand had broken through the skin of the pumpkin. He had pulled it out again, and was looking at it. Pumpkin pulp dripped from his fingers in big sticky blobs, and his skin was covered in juice.

"Oh, no," he said. "Get it off me! Get it off me!"

I didn't know what the big deal was about a little vegetable juice, but seeing the man with pumpkin on his hand seemed to upset the other workers. Two of them ran over to him with rags and started to wipe the juice away as quickly as they could. The others stood around watching anxiously. No one seemed to notice me watching them.

The two men wiping the pumpkin juice finished working on the man and stepped away.

"He's going to have to go to decontamination," said one of the men. "We didn't get it off quickly enough."

The man who had gotten juiced started to blubber. "No," he said. "No. I'm fine. Don't make me go there. Don't make me."

The other men were all looking away from their co-worker. Then two more men appeared. They were wearing special suits with big protective gloves and face masks.

"Come on, Pete," one of them said to the man who was crying. "You know the rules."

"But I'm fine!" Pete said, backing away from them.

"You know that's not true," said one of the men. "You've been contaminated. Now let's get you out of here before anyone else gets it."

They started to lead Pete toward the barn. They were coming toward me, and I didn't want them to know I'd seen what had happened. I ducked behind a pile of Eerie Farms boxes and watched them go by. As Pete passed me, I snuck a glimpse of his hand. When I saw what had happened, it was all I could do not to scream.

All over his hand and arm, where the pumpkin juice had splashed him, Pete's skin was covered with a green rash. The same green rash I had on my arm and that Simon had on his leg.

*B*efore I could get a really good look at Pete's rash, the two men led him away. But just from the quick glimpse, I knew that it was the same rash I had on my arm. It was the same green color, and it had the same slightly fuzzy texture to it. Only Pete's rash covered all of his hand and most of his arm. It was everywhere the pumpkin juice had touched him.

I leaned against the wall behind the packing crates and tried to focus my thoughts. I'd seen Pete's skin coated in the sticky pumpkin juice. Then a few minutes later it had been covered in the mysterious rash. There was obviously some kind of connection. And the other men had been terrified to touch him or to get near the juice, so they must have known that there was something dangerous about it.

I rolled up my sleeve and looked at the rash on my arm. It had stopped spreading, but the green color had deepened, and the texture was becoming softer, almost like there was mold growing on my skin. I touched the spot and felt my stomach get a little queasy. Then I tried to think back to the night before the rash had appeared. I remembered biting into one of the peas and having it spurt a little bit of juice onto my arm. I'd wiped it away with a napkin, and hadn't thought anything of it. But now I had this rash.

My first thought was that I had to run and tell Bud and my father what had happened. Maybe they could stop people from eating the vegetables and coming into contact with the juice. But then I remembered how the men loading the pumpkin into the truck already knew it was dangerous. That's when I really got scared. Because if Bud and the other people at Eerie Farms already knew about the dangers of their produce, then it meant that they were letting people get infected with whatever was causing the rash. It meant they were doing it on purpose.

But why? What possible reason could they have for wanting people in Eerie to get green rashes? It didn't make any sense.

My second thought was that I should have followed Pete and the two men to see where they were taking him and what they were going to do to him. But they were already gone. Besides, I had been away from the cafeteria for a long time. If I didn't get back, Bud might start to get suspicious, and I didn't want to cause any trouble. At least not until I found out a little more about what was going on around Eerie Farms.

Making sure that there was no one around to see me,

I came out from behind the boxes and ran back to the cafeteria. Before I went inside, I took a deep breath to settle myself. Then I opened the door and looked around for my dad, Simon, and Bud.

They were sitting at a table near a window. They each had a big bowl of beets in front of them, and they were eating hungrily. When they saw me standing in the doorway, Bud waved me over.

"Thought we lost you there, pal," he said when I came over.

"It just took me longer than I thought to find my hat," I said. "It had blown under a truck, and I couldn't see it."

"Have some of these beets," my dad said. "They're out of this world."

I looked at the bowl of shiny red beets, and I felt sick. They were sitting in a little pool of juice, and all I could think of was how Pete had sounded so terrified when he'd gotten the pumpkin juice on himself.

"Go on, Marshall, try one," Bud urged. "They're good for you."

I picked up a fork and stabbed one of the beets with it. I lifted it out of the bowl, and some of the juice dripped from the bottom onto the table top. I couldn't help but notice that when Bud saw the juice he pulled his arm away and quickly wiped up the red drops with his napkin.

I didn't want to put that beet in my mouth, but I knew I had to. I didn't want to embarrass my dad, who was watching me expectantly. Closing my eyes so I wouldn't have to look at it, I popped the beet into my mouth and started chewing. It was delicious, but I could barely taste it because I couldn't get the sight of Pete's rash-covered skin out of my head.

"Aren't they great?" said Simon when I swallowed. He was eating everything in his bowl as quickly as he could. His mouth and chin were stained red with beet juice. He raised his hand to his lips to wipe it away.

"No!" I shouted, grabbing his hand. "Don't do that."

I looked around and saw that everyone in the cafeteria was looking at me with puzzled expressions.

"Um . . . I mean, don't use your hand," I said, fumbling for an excuse. "You should . . . um . . . use a napkin."

I handed Simon a napkin, and he wiped his mouth. I knew he was confused, but I couldn't explain to him right then why I had stopped him from touching the beet juice. It would have to wait.

"Are you okay, Marshall?" my dad asked.

"Sure," I said. "I'm fine. Why wouldn't I be fine? I just didn't want Simon to stain his hands or anything."

"Gee, thanks, Mom," said Simon sarcastically, and everyone laughed. I could feel myself turning as red as, well, a beet, but I knew that I'd just saved my best friend from giving himself one big rash.

"Have some more beets," Bud said, handing me a heaping bowl of them.

I didn't want to eat any more beets. In fact, I didn't want to eat anything at all that was grown at Eerie Farms. But with everyone watching me, I didn't have much choice. While Dad, Bud, and Simon talked about the farm, I ate a few of the beets. But when no one was looking, I dumped them into my napkin and hid the whole mess in a basket of rolls sitting on the table.

When everyone else was done eating, my father said it was time for us to go. We all went outside with Bud and said good-bye.

"Thanks for the tour," Simon said, shaking Bud's hand. "It was really great to see where all of this stuff comes from."

"My pleasure," said Bud. "I'm always proud to show off what we've accomplished here. And Marshall, it was good to meet you. Maybe one day you'll follow in your dad's footsteps and help the world see just what fine things we have here in Eerie, Indiana."

"Maybe," I said, thinking that if anyone ever saw even half the things I'd seen in Eerie, they'd run screaming for the hills.

We got into the car and drove away from Eerie Farms. Dad waved to the guards at the gate as though they were his best friends, and they waved back. I was really quiet the whole way home, but Dad and Simon were talking so much about what we'd seen that they never even noticed that I barely said three words.

When we got back to my house, Simon and I went up into the Secret Spot, where our Evidence Locker is.

As soon as the door was closed, I sat Simon down and told him everything I'd seen when I went back for my hat. I'd been holding it in for so long that I let it all out in one long rush, barely stopping to breathe.

"So I think that's what's causing our rashes," I said when I was finished.

Simon just sat there looking at me in disbelief. Then he looked down at the small green spot on his leg.

"I did spill some juice from the broccoli on myself," he said. "But how could vegetable juice cause a rash? That's ridiculous."

"Like you said before, we could be allergic to it," I said. "But I don't think that's it."

Simon groaned. "I know where this is headed," he said. "This is going to turn into some big mystery, isn't it? Even the *food* in Eerie is weird."

"Yeah, but that's not the scariest thing," I said. "If the juice can do this to our outsides, imagine what it's doing to our insides."

Simon's stomach started to growl, and he put his hands on it. "I don't even want to think about that," he said. "If my insides are all covered in green mold, I think I'd just rather not know."

"Whatever is causing this is inside the vegetables," I said. "And I think it's being put there on purpose by the people at Eerie Farms."

"Okay, but what is it?" said Simon. "And why would they want to go around giving people rashes? That doesn't make any sense."

"Does most of what happens in Eerie make sense?" I said.

"I guess you're right. By now I should be used to this kind of stuff. But what do we do now? Should we tell your dad?"

I shook my head. "He wouldn't believe us," I said. "Just like the time we tried to tell him about what we found buried in the garden. Besides, there's still the chance that I'm wrong about this. If that's true, then I don't want to jeopardize his job. This project is too important to him for me to screw it up."

"Let me get this straight," said Simon. "We have these strange rashes, but we don't really know why. We think there *might* be something weird going on at Eerie Farms, but we have no way of finding out. And your dad is smack in the middle of it all, but we aren't going to tell him anything?"

"Right," I said. "Look, I know it sounds stupid, but we just don't know enough yet, okay?"

"So we're just supposed to sit around getting greener and greener until someone tells us something?"

"No," I said. "We're going to take action."

"Like what?"

I thought. "For one thing," I said firmly, "we're going to stop eating vegetables."

"Stop eating vegetables?" said Simon. "How are we going to get away with that? All my mom makes these days is vegetables."

"I know," I said. "My mom is doing the same thing.

But we have to stop eating them. We don't know what they're doing to us, but we know it's probably pretty bad. So the only thing we can do is just not eat anything that's grown at Eerie Farms."

"Looks like we'll be making a lot of secret trips to Burger Chef," said Simon.

"It won't be so bad," I said. "You'll just have to say you're eating at my house, and I'll say I'm eating at your house. Then we can go get food that's safe to eat."

"How do we know this isn't just happening to us?" said Simon. "I haven't exactly seen people running around with green spots on them. Have you?"

"No," I admitted. "But maybe the people who *do* have them are covering them up like we are. And maybe they're all wondering why they have the spots, too. There could be a lot of people in Eerie who are contaminated, and we'd never even know it."

"And how do we find out exactly what *is* going on?" asked Simon.

"We have to go back to Eerie Farms," I said. "When Pete was being led away, I heard them talking about taking him for decontamination. I bet if we go back we can find out what they're up to."

"But how do we get in? You saw the guards at the gate. There's no way we'd get past them again."

I thought for a minute. Then I had an idea. "You're right," I said. "There's no way we could get past that gate if they saw us. But what if they don't see us?"

"What do you mean?" said Simon. "You have that look on your face."

"What look?" I said innocently.

"The one that says we're going to be getting ourselves into a whole lot of trouble pretty soon," he said. "I'd know that look anywhere."

"I was just thinking," I said. "The only way in and out of Eerie Farms is in a car, right?"

"Or if you're a vegetable," said Simon jokingly.

"Exactly," I said.

Simon looked puzzled. "I don't get it."

"We're going to become vegetables," I said.

"I think you might already be one," said Simon. "I still don't get it."

"Every day trucks go in and out of that place carrying produce to the markets," I explained. "The guards never check them because they know what's in them."

"So if we're inside one of them, they'll never see us," said Simon. "Now I get it."

"The truck delivers to Eerie Greens Market at the same time every morning," I said. "If we can get into the back of it, we can get a free ride all the way to Eerie Farms, and no one will ever know."

"And if anyone looks inside, we just have to pretend to be cabbages," said Simon.

For the rest of the afternoon, we planned how we were going to get onto the Eerie Farms truck the next morning. Then it was time for Simon to go home. After he left, I went into the kitchen and got a big glass of water from the tap. I drank it quickly and filled the glass again. As I took it back to my room, I found myself wondering once more why I was so thirsty all the time.

I feel like a plant that needs watering, I thought as I stretched out on my bed to take a nap before dinner.

5

The next morning, Sunday, my parents slept in late, so it was easy for me to sneak out of the house and meet Simon. Besides, the sun hadn't even come up yet, and there was no one out on the streets except for the truck drivers delivering fresh doughnuts and Sunday papers to World of Stuff and the Eerie Diner, and they were so tired they didn't even notice two kids walking down Main Street.

When we got to Eerie Greens, Simon and I looked around for a place to hide. The owner of the store, Mrs. Pamplemousse, was fussing around outside, arranging and rearranging the apples and the bunches of dill. She didn't take any notice of us as we slipped around to the back of the store and hid behind a pile of boxes waiting to be recycled.

"How are we going to get onto the truck?" asked Simon as we waited.

"When the guy unloads the crates of vegetables, we'll

have a few seconds while his back is turned to run into the truck,'' I said.

"What if there isn't anywhere to hide?" said Simon.

"Then we get caught," I said.

Before Simon could say anything else, the Eerie Farms truck pulled up outside the back door of the market. The driver got out and opened the back of the truck. He climbed inside, and a minute later he came back out carrying a big box of carrots. He went over to the door of Eerie Greens and opened it.

"Okay," I said, pushing Simon toward the truck. "Now's our chance."

We scrambled for the back of the truck and dove inside. The truck was filled with all kinds of vegetables in boxes, and it was dark.

"I can't see anywhere to hide," said Simon.

"Way up front," I said, pointing at a pile of lumpy objects. "I bet those are potatoes. We can hide behind the sacks."

Outside, I could hear the Eerie Farms delivery man whistling as he came back to the truck for another box. We didn't have much time left. I ran to the sacks of potatoes and crouched behind them. Simon was right beside me, and we were barely hidden by the tops of the bags.

The man climbed into the truck and started looking around. He was talking to Mrs. Pamplemousse, who was standing outside the truck.

"Need any squash today?" he said.

"Oh, yes," said Mrs. Pamplemousse. "Squash, peas, beans, tomatoes, and broccoli."

The man grabbed boxes of the things that Mrs. Pamplemousse wanted and piled them near the opening of the truck. Then he got out and carried them into the store for her. I breathed a sigh of relief as he picked up the last one and took it in. Then he came back and started to shut the truck door.

"Just a minute," said Mrs. Pamplemousse before the door clicked shut. "I almost forgot—I need a big bag of potatoes. Everyone has been asking for them."

"Sure thing," said the man. "Coming right up."

He came into the truck and walked toward the pile of potatoes that we were hiding behind. My heart started racing as he reached for the sack right in front of me. If he moved it, I would be exposed. I watched, terrified, as his fingers closed around the edge.

"Never mind," Mrs. Pamplemousse called out just as the man was lifting up the bag. "I forgot I still have a bag from yesterday."

The man sighed and let go of the bag. My heart slowed down, and I looked at Simon. His eyes were closed, but when he heard the man leave, he opened them again.

"Sorry," he whispered. "I just couldn't watch."

This time the man closed the door of the truck for real. Then he climbed into the front and started the engine. The truck lurched out onto the street, and we were on our way.

"I guess we should stay hidden," I said. "In case he makes any more stops."

Luckily for us, he didn't make any more deliveries. The truck drove right out of town and turned onto Route 13. A little while later, we turned off onto what I knew from the bumpy ride was the dirt road leading to Eerie Farms. After a quick stop at the gate, the truck went a little further and then came to a stop. The man got out, shut his door, and left.

"I guess he isn't going to unload the truck," said Simon when three or four minutes had gone by and no one opened the back door.

We stood up and stretched. Crouching behind the sacks of potatoes had made my legs hurt, and it felt good to be able to move them a little. When they had returned to normal, I went to the door of the truck and pulled the handle. Pushing it open a crack, I peeked outside. We were parked behind the big barn.

"There's no one out there," I said to Simon. "Let's go."

We jumped out of the truck and ran for the barn doors. I figured that whatever we were looking for, it was probably in there, since that's where the two men had taken Pete after he was covered in pumpkin juice. When we got to the doors, I opened one and we slipped inside.

While the outside of the Eerie Farms barn looked just like any old barn, the inside was something else. It looked like a high-tech laboratory. There were rows of gleaming metal tables along one wall, and on one side was a giant tank filled with what I guessed was the fertilizer they used on the vegetables. Bright lights shone down on trays of plants, and several computers were humming and whirring.

I started to walk around the barn, looking at everything. It felt like I was inside the control room of a space center, not in the barn of a vegetable farm. Simon followed behind me.

"What is all this?" he said. "I thought we were going to find bags of manure and maybe a tractor or two."

"I have no idea what this stuff is," I said. "But something tells me there's more going on here than just gardening."

At one end of the barn, we came to a door marked DECONTAMINATION AREA. There was a big black skull painted on the door.

"What do you think is through there?" said Simon. I tried the handle of the door, but it was locked.

"I guess we're not going to find out," I said.

I turned back to the main room. I had no idea what I was looking for or where to start. Finally, I walked over to one of the computers and looked at it. It was already turned on, and the screen showed lists of files. I scanned the file names: Planting Records, Crop Yields, Hybridization Charts, Pruning Schedule. None of them looked particularly interesting. Then, at the bottom, I saw a file called Eerie Germination Plan Report.

"What could that be?" said Simon, reading over my shoulder.

"Let's find out," I said, clicking on the file.

There was some humming and whirring as the file opened, and then the screen showed the following readout:

The Eerie Germination Plan is going much better than predicted. The experimental DNA engineering procedure has resulted in a fertilizer that affects the cell growth of the plants and produces unusually large and flavorful produce. While there have been some visible side effects resulting from exposure to treated produce, we are confident that with further testing we will be able to control the effects of the fertilizer completely and make them totally unnoticeable.

"They're experimenting with changing the DNA of plants," I said.

"What does that mean?" asked Simon. "It all sounds like nonsense to me."

I knew a little bit about DNA because we'd studied it in science class the year before. I tried to explain it to Simon so he would understand.

"DNA is what makes something grow the way it's supposed to," I said. "Your DNA is what determines what you'll look like—what color hair you'll have, how tall you are, all of that stuff. You get part of your DNA from your mother and part of it from your father."

"And plants have DNA, too?" he said.

"Right," I said. "By changing a person's—or I guess a plant's—DNA, you can change what it looks like. By combining DNA from the healthiest plants, they can get plants that are bigger and stronger."

"Or taste better," added Simon. "So that's why the Eerie Farms produce is so big and tastes so good."

I nodded. "They found a way to change the DNA in the plants to make super vegetables."

"That doesn't sound so awful," said Simon.

"Not by itself," I said. "But they seem to be having problems controlling what they're doing. See, it mentions side effects from exposure to the vegetables."

I continued to read the information on the computer screen.

The most common side effect reported by our researchers is a green rash caused as a result of being exposed to the juices of plants treated with the fertilizer. While the rash is generally restricted to a small spot on the skin, several more severe cases have been reported. We are currently keeping two such cases under quarantine in order to study them and perhaps find an antidote to the rash.

I thought about Pete, and how his whole arm had been covered in the rash. I wondered if he was one of the cases being studied, or if there were people with even worse rashes. If there were, I didn't want to see them. But there was more to read.

While we are pleased with the rate at which the produce, and thus the fertilizer, is being consumed by the population of Eerie, we feel it is necessary to speed up the rate of exposure. To this end, we are experimenting with several additional means of introducing the fertilizer into the general population.

"What's that all about?" said Simon. "What do they mean about exposing the population of Eerie to the fertilizer?"

"It sounds like they want people to get this stuff into their bodies," I said. "But why would they want to do that, especially if they know there are side effects?"

"And how are they doing it?" said Simon. "I mean, besides making sure the vegetables are loaded with it."

Before I could read any more of the computer file, the door to the barn swung open. I quickly turned off the computer, and Simon and I hid beneath one of the tables.

"So the truck is all filled up, right?" said a man's voice.

"Yep," said a second voice. "It's all set."

"Good," said the first man. "You know where to go, then?"

"Yep," the second man said again.

"Make sure no one sees you. We can't have anyone getting suspicious."

I looked over the edge of the table and saw the two men. One of them was Bud, the man who had shown us around Eerie Farms the day before. The other man was wearing an Eerie Farms uniform, but I didn't recall seeing him before.

After grabbing some papers from one of the tables, the two men left the barn, and Simon and I came out from behind the table. I really wanted to get another look at the computer file, but something told me I should follow Bud and the other guy. I went to the door and looked out. The man was getting into an unmarked truck. Bud was nowhere in sight.

"We have to get on that truck," I said to Simon. "Follow me."

As the truck started to pull away, I ran behind it and jumped onto the back step. I pulled open the door and climbed in. When I looked out, Simon was running behind the truck, trying to keep up.

"Grab my hand," I said, reaching down.

Simon's fingers closed around mine, and I gave a big pull. He jumped into the truck, and I fell backwards. He fell on top of me.

"Thanks," he said, rolling off.

"No problem," I said. "But next time, try not to land so hard."

Unlike the first Eerie Farms truck we'd been in that day, this one was filled with big plastic barrels. Each one had the word FERTILIZER painted on it in red letters.

"What do you think he's doing with them?" Simon said.

"We're just going to have to wait and find out," I said.

We sat down and waited for the ride to end. The driver took the usual route out the gate and down the dirt road. But when he came to Route 13, he turned right instead of left.

"He's not going into town," said Simon.

"He's going toward Lake Eerie," I said. "What could he want out there?"

"I don't know," said Simon as the truck hit a bump, "but I'm starting to know how a package must feel after riding around in a mail truck all day."

The truck rumbled on, making several turns before coming to a stop. The driver got out and came around to the back. Simon and I were hiding behind the last row of barrels, and he didn't see us as he opened the door and rolled one of the barrels off.

We heard him pushing the barrel through what sounded like grass, and we went to the back to see what he was doing. We got out and hid behind some trees. Sure enough, we were at Lake Eerie. The water was shining blue and clean in the morning sun. I even saw a few fish jumping out of the water, trying to catch the bugs that hovered above the surface.

The man pushed the barrel to the water's edge. Then he put on a pair of heavy rubber gloves that went way up his arms. Lifting the lid of the barrel, he leaned it over. Bright green liquid poured from the top and into the water of Lake Eerie.

"Oh, no," I said, watching the green stain spread out across the water.

"What?" said Simon. "What's he doing?"

I looked at him. "I think I know how they're planning on getting the fertilizer into our systems," I said.

"What are you talking about?" said Simon.
"The water," I said. "Eerie's water comes out of Lake Eerie. What better way to make sure everyone is exposed to whatever that stuff is than by putting it into the water?"

Suddenly Simon realized what I was saying. "You mean every time anyone gets a drink of water or takes a shower . . ."

"He or she is coming into contact with those chemicals," I said.

Simon leaned against a tree. He looked pale. "That means every single person in Eerie could be infected," he said. "But why would they want everyone in Eerie to get a rash?"

"I think it's more than just a rash," I said. "I don't know what it is, but something tells me that this isn't just some skin condition we're dealing with."

I looked at the patch of green on my arm. Since I'd

stopped eating the vegetables, it hadn't grown any larger. But it hadn't gotten any smaller, either.

"We have to tell people," said Simon. "We have to warn them. We don't know how long they've been dumping this stuff into the water. The whole town might be contaminated already."

"I agree," I said. "But we have to do it carefully, and we have to make sure we don't expose ourselves to any more of that . . . that . . . stuff."

"And just how will we do that?" asked Simon.

"We have to stop washing," I said. "And we can't drink any water."

"Stop washing?" said Simon. "We're going to stink."

"That's just a chance we'll have to take," I said.

The man was coming back from dumping the chemicals into the lake. Simon and I ran off into the trees so he wouldn't see us. I wasn't exactly sure of our location, but we'd searched around Lake Eerie enough times looking for Bigfoot and other stuff that I knew we could find our way home. We just kept pushing our way through the trees until we came to the road that led to Route 13.

We were walking down that road when we heard someone coming. I looked behind us and saw the truck from Eerie Farms driving along the road.

"Should we run?" said Simon.

"Just act natural," I said as the truck pulled up alongside us and slowed down.

"Hi, boys," the driver said. "What are you doing out here today?" He was being really friendly, but I knew I couldn't trust him.

"Um, we're doing some bird-watching," I said.

"Yeah," added Simon. "We're looking for a blue-horned screech thrush."

"Screech thrush?" said the man. "They rare?"

"They sure are," I said. "You're lucky if you ever see one in your lifetime."

The man laughed. "Well, you need a lift home or anything?"

"No, thanks," I said. "We're going to look around a little bit more."

The man nodded. "Have fun," he said. "If you get too hot, you can always take a swim in the lake."

I thought about him dumping all of those chemicals into the water. I could tell by the tone of his voice that he *wanted* us to go swimming. I shivered.

"Maybe," I said.

The man waved good-bye and took off down the road again, leaving a cloud of dirt behind.

"Did you hear that?" said Simon. "He was trying to get us into that water."

I looked down at myself. I was all grimy from riding around in the trucks and walking through the woods. So was Simon. Our skin and clothes were covered in dirt, and we were all sweaty from running around.

"I wish we could get in the water," I said. "It's going to be impossible to get clean now."

"But we can just take show . . ." Simon began, then realized what he was saying. "Oh, no," he moaned. "How will we get clean?"

"We'll just have to wipe as much off as we can," I said as we continued walking. "Until we know for sure what's going on, all water is off limits."

We finally reached the main road and started to make our way back to Eerie. The sun had come out, and we had to walk for several miles. By the time we got back to our street, we were both tired and filthy.

First we stopped at my house. When we went into the kitchen, my mother was chopping up vegetables for a salad.

"Oh, there you are," she said. "I was wondering where you were this morning." She didn't seem to notice that I was dirty at all.

"We went for a walk," I said.

"That's nice. You're just in time for lunch. We're having salad and vegetable soup. Homemade. Simon, you can stay if you want to."

"We can't," I said quickly, eyeing the tomato my mom was cutting up. She hadn't even washed it, and there were little pieces of dirt clinging to the sides. "I mean, we already had lunch at Simon's. Say, aren't you going to wash that first?"

My mother picked up a piece of tomato and popped it into her mouth, dirt and all. "Why?" she said. "A little dirt never hurt anyone. In fact, I seem to recall reading somewhere that it's even good for you."

Something weird was going on. I looked at my mom's face as she ate. "Have your eyes always been green?" I asked her. Her eyes were peculiarly bright, almost the color of leaves.

"Of course," she said, eating another slice of tomato. "What a funny question to ask. Are you sure you don't want something to eat?"

I decided to try another approach. "Don't you think maybe we're having too many vegetables these days?" I said. "I mean, couldn't we have hamburgers or something?"

My mother laughed. "Why would you want to eat a hamburger?" she said. "These vegetables are so much better. Why, ever since we've been eating them, I feel like my whole body is growing. I'm a completely different person."

I could see that arguing with her wasn't going to get me anywhere. She was determined to keep eating the Eerie Farms produce, and there was nothing I could do about it.

"Okay," I said. "We're just going to go upstairs now."

"We'll be outside if you change your mind about lunch," she said.

"Outside?"

"It's so nice out," she answered. "I feel like being in the sun today. We're going to have a picnic in the backyard."

Something was definitely weird. My family never

went on picnics except on Tornado Day, and that was a whole month away. For my mom to be eating outside, something had to be severely odd.

Simon and I went up to the Secret Spot and I closed the door. I went to the window closest to the Evidence Locker and looked out. In the backyard, my father and Syndi were sunning themselves on beach chairs. They were both drinking big glasses of water, and their bare feet were resting in the grass.

"I don't know what those chemicals are doing," I said. "But we've got to find out soon. My whole family has gone crazy."

"They were a little bit off before this," said Simon, watching as my dad turned on the hose and started watering the lawn.

"I know," I said. "But this is ridiculous. Look, he's trying to water Syndi now."

It was true. My father had aimed the hose right at Syndi. The water was splashing over her feet, and she was laughing like crazy.

"I *am* kind of hungry," said Simon. "Where can we get something to eat that isn't vegetables?"

I thought about it for a minute. Now my father was holding the hose up in the air and my mom was running through the water.

"I guess we could go to World of Stuff for an ice-cream sundae," I said.

Simon grinned. "Now that's my kind of lunch," he said. "I could really get into this no-vegetables thing."

We left my family watering each other in the backyard and went downtown to World of Stuff. There were a few people in there, looking at the new shipment of garden gnomes Mr. Radford had just gotten in, but the stools at the soda fountain were empty. Simon and I took our usual seats and waited for Mr. Radford to come over.

"Well, hello there," he said when he noticed us waiting. "What are you two up to today? From the looks of it, I'd say you've been wrestling wild pigs or something. Look at all that dirt."

"No, Mr. Radford," I said. "We were just—um—working in the garden. You know, digging in the dirt. I guess most of it ended up on us."

"I'll say," said Mr. Radford. "You look like a couple of sunburned snowmen." He thought his joke was really funny, and started laughing. I waited for him to stop.

"Actually, we just came in for some sundaes," I said.

"Well, this is the place," he said. "What will it be? Peanut butter with hot fudge, cherry chunk with butterscotch, or maybe marshmallow delight with pecans."

"I think I'll have just plain old vanilla with chocolate sprinkles," I said.

"And I'll have strawberry with caramel," said Simon.

"Ah, traditionalists," said Mr. Radford. "My kind of people. Coming right up."

As Mr. Radford scooped the ice cream and put the toppings on, I decided to ask him a few questions. He usually knew everything that was going on in Eerie, even if he often didn't remember it from day to day.

"So, Mr. Radford," I said. "What do you think of these new vegetables everyone is so excited about?"

"Vegetables?" he said. "Who eats vegetables? Why, when I was a young man, we ate nothing but meat, day in and day out. Vegetables? Nonsense."

"So, you haven't tried them?" Simon said as Mr. Radford put his sundae down in front of him and handed him a spoon.

"Not on your life," he said. "You wouldn't see me going near a plate of spinach. Why, the only reason I belong to the Loyal Order of Corn is so I can wear the nifty hat."

Mr. Radford finished putting the chocolate sprinkles on top of my ice cream and handed me the dish. I picked up my spoon and took a big spoonful. It was wonderful to be eating something that wasn't a vegetable, and I let the ice cream melt in my mouth and run over my tongue. It tasted so good that for a moment I let myself believe that everything really was all right in Eerie. Maybe I was making a big deal out of nothing. Maybe the green rash was harmless, something that would go away in a few days.

Mr. Radford was busy looking for something behind the counter. When he came back up, he was holding two dishes of what looked like mint ice cream. He put them down in front of us.

"How would you boys like to try a sample of my

newest flavor?'' he said. ''I think it's going to be very popular. I just got it yesterday, and I haven't been able to stop eating it.''

I took a bite of the ice cream and tasted it. It was really good—very sweet and a little tart at the same time. I couldn't quite place the taste.

''This is great,'' said Simon. ''What is it, rhubarb or something?''

Mr. Radford shook his head. ''Guess again,'' he said.

''Kiwi?'' I tried.

''Wrong again,'' he said.

''Okay, tell us,'' said Simon. He had eaten almost the whole dish, and was lifting the last spoonful to his mouth.

''It's okra,'' he said.

''Okra?'' I said. ''But that's a vegetable.''

Mr. Radford winked. ''Exactly,'' he said.

''But I thought you said you didn't eat vegetables,'' said Simon, the spoon of okra ice cream still in his hand.

''But this isn't vegetables,'' said Mr. Radford. ''It's ice cream. And who doesn't like ice cream?''

I was starting to get a sinking feeling. ''Did you make this yourself?'' I asked him.

''No,'' he said. ''Fellow over at Eerie Farms came up with it. Asked me if I'd try it out for him. Some new thing they're working on. Pretty smart, eh?''

I looked at Simon. He had a sick look on his face. He had put the spoon of ice cream down and was staring at it.

"This is going to be big, I tell you," Mr. Radford was saying. "Big. Everyone in town will be asking for this stuff."

He was leaning on the counter as he talked, and all of a sudden I noticed something in his hair. Something green. I looked closer, and saw that there was a long piece of what looked like grass curling out from behind his ear. Then I looked again and saw that it wasn't grass at all. It was a tendril, like the kind a pea plant would send out while it was growing. It had wrapped around his ear and was growing down the side of his face.

"Mr. Radford," I said. "Exactly how much of this ice cream have you eaten since yesterday?"

"Oh, I don't know," he said. "A gallon. Maybe two. It's good stuff. Why?"

"No reason," I said, staring at the tendril behind his ear. A horrible thought had come to me, a thought so terrible I couldn't even bring myself to say it. But as I looked at that bit of green in Mr. Radford's hair, I knew that what I was thinking was true.

He was turning into a plant.

7

All at once, everything came together in my mind, like the pieces of a jigsaw puzzle suddenly arranging themselves into a complete picture. Seeing the tendril growing out of Mr. Radford's hair made everything clear—well, almost. But I couldn't say anything with Mr. Radford right there, so I grabbed Simon's elbow.

"Come on," I said, practically pulling him off his stool. "There's something we have to do. Right now."

"Hey!" said Simon. "What gives?"

"We'll see you later, Mr. Radford," I said as I pulled Simon out the door of World of Stuff. "Thanks for the ice cream."

"My pleasure," he said. "Come again. I'm told we'll have broccoli sorbet next week!"

Once we were out on the street, I told Simon what I'd seen.

"He's turning into a *plant*?" said Simon incredulously. "Are you crazy?"

"Think about it," I said. "Those chemicals that they're using on the vegetables at Eerie Farms—they work by changing the plants' DNA, right?"

"Sure, if you say so," said Simon. "I still don't quite get that part."

"Just trust me," I said. "So if they're pouring those same chemicals into the Eerie water supply, then people are being exposed to them, right?"

"Right," said Simon. "That part I get."

"Well, maybe those chemicals are doing something to the DNA of *people*. Maybe, somehow, the plant DNA and the human DNA are getting all mixed up."

"So people are becoming plants?" said Simon. "That's impossible."

"So are UFOs and Bigfoot and plastic kitchenware that keeps you alive forever," I said. "At least, that's what everyone tries to tell us. But we know all of that stuff exists in Eerie."

Simon thought about this for a minute. "You're right," he said. "I still don't understand how it all works, but I believe it."

"The question is, why would anyone do it?" I said.

"Maybe they don't know," said Simon.

"Oh, they know," I said. "Remember that report we found on the computer? It said they were looking for ways to introduce the fertilizer into the general population. Well, that general population is everyone in Eerie."

"And we don't know how long they've been doing

it," said Simon. "It could have been going on for weeks."

"I don't think it's been that long," I said. "The rash didn't show up on us until this week, and since we stopped eating vegetables it hasn't spread. Mr. Radford has been eating the okra ice cream, and he's also probably been exposed to the contaminated water, so there's more of the chemical in his body."

"What do you think it will do to him?" asked Simon.

"I don't know," I said. "But I don't think I want to find out. We have to stop this."

"How?"

"I think it's time we told my dad," I said. "I know he's never believed us before, but he's working on the Eerie Farms account. Maybe he can get his boss to investigate."

"We don't really have much of a choice, do we?" Simon said. "Everyone else would just think we were nuts."

"As usual," I said.

We walked back to my house, rehearsing how we would tell my dad about what we'd seen at Eerie Farms. I knew he was going to be upset that we'd trespassed on private property, and he'd probably say we were putting his job in danger. But if we could just get him to listen to us, I knew he'd have to believe us. Or even if he didn't believe us, his logical brain would be curious enough to look into it.

On the way we realized how thirsty we were. We

stopped at the supermarket and got enough soda and bottled water to last the next few days.

When we got home, I checked the backyard first. Syndi was still sunbathing on her towel, and my mom was digging in the dirt. She was planting something, and her hands were pushed right into the soil. My dad was nowhere to be seen.

"What are you doing?" I asked my mother.

"I had this sudden urge to dig in the dirt," she said. "It feels so good on my skin."

Almost more than anything else, my mother hates to get her hands dirty. Whenever she gets anything under her fingernails, she scrubs them like crazy. Now she was sitting there in the grass, soil all over her skin.

"What are you planting?" I said.

"Oh, I don't really know," she answered. "You know how I am with plants. I can't even keep plastic flowers from wilting. These are just some plants your father brought home from work. I thought they might be pretty."

I looked at the little plants, imagining what kinds of chemicals were swirling around in their tiny leaves. I wanted to rip them right out of the ground, but I knew my mother would freak out if I did. She was obviously under the influence of the Eerie Farms produce. Then I remembered that the whole family had been playing in the water from the hose when I left. Who knew what had gotten into them?

"Speaking of Dad," I said, "where is he?"

"He had to go to the office," my mother said.

"On a Sunday?" I said.

She nodded. "Mr. Plante called and said there was some big project they had to do, and he needed your father's help."

"Did he say when he'd be back?"

"No. He just said not to wait up. I think this might take a while. Is there something you needed to talk to him about? You know you can always talk to me, Marshall."

"Thanks, Mom," I said. "This isn't important. I just wanted to ask him about some—um—chemistry homework I have."

"Well, I never was very good at chemistry," she said.

"That's okay," I said. "It can wait."

"Why don't you boys go in and have a snack?" my mother suggested. "I think there's some leftover vegetable stew in the fridge."

She sniffed the air, her nose all wrinkled up. "On second thought," she said, "maybe you should take showers first. I hate to say it, but you boys don't smell so fresh."

Simon and I hightailed it out of there before she could ask us any questions. We went up to the Secret Spot, shut the door, and sat down.

"Do you think we should go over to your dad's office?" said Simon after we'd thought about what we should do.

"No," I said. "If he's there with his boss, we won't

be able to talk to him. We'll just have to wait until he comes home.''

"That's just until tomorrow morning," said Simon. "That should be okay. What could happen between now and then?''

"Not much, I guess. I don't think one more shower is going to hurt anyone now. The worst that will happen is that everyone in town will have vines growing out of their ears.''

"Or that Mr. Radford will start sprouting flowers," said Simon.

Even though we were in the middle of something really weird, that cracked us both up, and we laughed for a long time. When we calmed down, I reached into my desk drawer and pulled out some packages of Wet Wipes hand washers I'd saved from the time my dad took us all out for lobster. I'd kept them, figuring they might come in handy for camping trips or something.

"Here," I said, handing a couple to Simon. "If we can't take showers, we might as well try washing with these.''

I ripped the top off the packet and pulled out the little moist towel inside. I unfolded it and started wiping my face with it.

"How do I look?'' I asked Simon.

"Well, the dirt is sort of streaked now. But you do look a little cleaner.''

"It will have to do," I said. I smelled like disinfectant from the stuff the towels were soaked in, and I felt a little sticky, but anything was an improvement over the dust that was all over me after being in the hot sun and walking down the dirt road from Lake Eerie.

Once we had both cleaned up as much as we could, Simon and I decided that we would walk back into town and maybe go to a movie. Since there was nothing we could do until we talked to my dad, we figured we could forget about things for a little while by seeing what was playing at the theater.

As it turned out, there was a double feature on: both old science fiction films. The first one was called *Pom-Pon Girls from Planet X*, and was all about aliens who masquerade as high-school cheerleaders. During a big performance at the homecoming football game, they all rip off their masks and reveal their true selves. The second movie, *Beyond the Beyond,* was about these two kids who find a way to travel back and forth in time. They try to go back in time and make things better, but when they come back to their real time, they find out that because of what they did, the world has been destroyed.

Both of the films were really good, but nothing compared to what Simon and I had seen in real life in Eerie. Still, eating two boxes of popcorn and a package of gummy fish *had* made me forget about the weird stuff going on at Eerie Farms.

At least until we left the theater and went back outside. When we pushed open the doors and walked out into the bright sunshine, the first thing we saw was a man in an Eerie Farms uniform plastering a poster on the wall by the theater. We walked over to look at it.

"What's going on?" I asked the man, who was just finishing rolling out the corners of the poster.

"See for yourself," he said, waving at the poster.

The poster showed a lot of happy people carrying giant vegetables in their arms. They were smiling and laughing as they walked through a field with their over-sized zucchinis, tomatoes, peas, corn, broccoli, and other veggies. Across the top of the poster were the words EERIE HARVEST DAYS.

"What is this?" asked Simon.

The man smiled. "It's a fair," he said. "We're going to hold a Harvest Days festival to celebrate the success of Eerie Farms. It starts on Friday and runs through the weekend. We're going to have games, rides, entertainment, and all kinds of things. It's going to be great."

"A whole festival for vegetables?" I said.

"Sure," the man said. "Eerie Farms is going to change the way this town lives, so we thought we might as well celebrate it."

As we'd been talking to the man, a small crowd had formed around the poster. People who had been out shopping or walking around came to see what was going on, and some of the people leaving the theater had stopped as well.

"I think it sounds great," said a woman who was holding her little girl's hand. "Just what this place needs."

I looked at the woman. She was wearing a big hat, but I could tell that underneath its brim her face was slightly green. Her little girl was twirling one of her pigtails around her finger, and running through her red hair I saw a thin green tendril.

"I just love Eerie Farms beans," said a man carrying several large Eerie Greens bags bursting with produce. "Why, I could eat them all day long."

"Well, you'll get your chance at the Harvest Days," said the man from Eerie Farms. "We'll have bean-eating contests, squash-eating contests, and every other kind of eating contest you can imagine."

"Oh, mommy," said the little girl with the tendril running through her pigtail. "Can we go? Can we go, please?"

"Of course we can, Daisy," said the woman. Then she beamed at everyone around her. "Daisy just *adores* her Eerie Farms vegetables. Why, I think if she eats one more carrot she's going to start sprouting leaves!"

"I think she already has," I muttered to Simon, and pointed at little Daisy's hair.

"That's just what we like to hear," said the Eerie Farms man. "We want to see all of Eerie come out to celebrate. It will be the biggest day in Eerie history. Why, we're even going to introduce a brand-new Eerie Farms vegetable product. It's the best yet."

There was a huge gasp from the crowd when the man made this announcement. I looked around me at all of the people. They were all smiling and laughing and talking about what it might be. As I watched their faces, most of which were tinged with some shade of green, I couldn't help but wonder if what was supposed to be the biggest day in Eerie's history might not turn out to be its *last* day.

8

When I got back to my house that night, I wanted more than anything to talk to my dad. Simon and I had experienced a lot of strange stuff in Eerie, and we'd always been able to handle it. But this was bigger than anything we'd ever faced before. It wasn't as if all we had to do was catch a werewolf or uncover an alien plot. We could do that in our sleep. This involved the whole town of Eerie. And to make things even worse, we didn't even know exactly what we were dealing with or how to fight it. We needed help.

But my dad wasn't home. All my mother said was that he was still at Things, Inc., working late with his boss. I tried calling him in his office, but the phone just rang and rang. The only thing I could do was go to bed and wait until morning. That night I slept horribly. I kept having dreams where I looked in the mirror and my face was covered in leaves.

When I finally woke up, it was daylight. I ran downstairs.

"Is Dad back yet?" I asked my mother. She was standing at the kitchen counter, feeding pieces of vegetables into her juice machine. A big glass pitcher was slowly filling up with the juice that poured out of the squeezer.

"Not yet, Mars," she said, dropping a chunk of turnip into the juicer. She didn't sound at all worried. "Want some juice? It's really great."

She poured a glass of the greenish brown juice and handed it to me. When she looked at me, I saw that her eyes were even greener than they'd been the day before, and that her eyebrows looked bushy and green, almost like overgrown hedges.

"No," I said. "I'm not thirsty. Do you know when Dad will be back?"

"He hasn't called," my mother said, taking a big gulp of the juice. "You sure you don't want some of this? It's delicious." She licked her lips, and I saw that her tongue was all green.

"Mom, have you seen your tongue?" I asked casually.

She stuck her tongue out and looked down at it.

"What do you know," she said. "It's green. I guess I've been drinking a lot of this juice."

"Don't you think that's sort of weird?" I asked. "I mean the green tongue and all."

"Not at all," she said. "A green tongue is a healthy tongue."

She was serious. She really did think that her having

a green tongue was perfectly normal. Whatever the chemicals in the vegetables and the water were doing to her body, they were also affecting her mind.

"I've got to get to school," I said. I had to go talk to Simon. We had to figure out something.

I backed out of the kitchen and almost ran right into Simon, who was coming to get me.

"Don't go in there," I said as he started to open the kitchen door.

"Why not?" he said. "Is your mom trying to cook pancakes again? I still remember the last time she did that. All that smoke . . ."

"No," I said. "She's not cooking. She's sort of turning, well, green."

Simon sighed. "Oh, no," he said. "Mine is acting weird, too. She keeps making cabbage muffins. She's eating them like crazy. So's my dad."

"I wish I could *find* my dad," I said. "He still hasn't turned up."

All we could do was go to school as usual. It was hard, especially since we still hadn't showered or anything. In English class, Charles Dodgson moved away from me, saying I smelled like I'd fallen down a rabbit hole, and when Simon and I met up at lunch, we had a whole table to ourselves. That was fine with us, especially since the lunch that day was stewed spinach and cauliflower. While everyone else ate it up and went back for more, we sat in the corner, eating the peanut butter and jelly sandwiches Simon had managed to make that morning while his mom wasn't looking. While we were busy checking out all the other kids for signs that they were becoming plants, we were getting some weird stares ourselves.

"Look at them," said a girl with the green rash all over her neck. "Can you believe they're actually eating something as disgusting as peanut butter and jelly?"

"They're so weird," said her friend, who was picking moss out from underneath her fingernails. "I heard they don't even water themselves properly."

The rest of the day was just as bad. Wherever I went, I saw kids who were in various states of becoming plant life. But no one seemed to think it was weird. They all thought I was the strange one. I couldn't wait for the day to end.

It finally did, but things didn't get any better. My father still wasn't home that night, and my mother and Syndi were too busy whipping up a lima bean upside-down cake to even notice. They were both turning progressively greener, and every time I looked at them I felt a little queasy.

My dad didn't come home on Tuesday. All my mom said was that he was working and would be home eventually. Finally, on Wednesday morning, I called his office again. This time, someone answered, but it wasn't my father. It was his boss, Mr. Plante.

"Hi," I said. "This is Marshall Teller. Is my dad there?"

"No," said Mr. Plante sharply. "I mean, he's here, but he can't come to the phone. He's kind of busy."

"Well, will you ask him to call me when he gets a chance?" I said. "It's kind of important."

"I'll tell him," said Mr. Plante. "But don't expect to hear from him for a while. He's up to his leaves . . . I mean neck . . . in work on the Eerie Farms account."

"Okay," I said. "Just tell him I called. Thanks."

I hung up and went to school. By now I smelled so bad that nobody would come near me. Simon was having the same problem. I found out because when I was sent to the principal's office, he was already waiting outside the door.

"You too, huh?" he said when he saw me walking down the hall.

"Mr. Pythagoras said he couldn't possibly teach us about obtuse angles because I stank," I said. "How about you?"

"I made an eighth-grader faint," Simon said. "She passed me in the hall on the way to recess and was knocked out cold."

I looked at the principal's door. I knew if we went in there we'd just end up getting sent home. It gave me an idea.

"What do you say we get out of here?" I said to Simon.

"And go where?" Simon said. "If we go home, they'll ask us why we aren't in school."

"We're not going home," I said. "We're going to go find my dad."

"But he's at work," said Simon.

"I know," I answered, walking toward the front doors. "We're going to Things, Incorporated."

Simon took one look back at the principal's door, then he followed me. We left school and started walking in the direction of Things, Inc., headquarters.

"How are we going to get in?" Simon said. "You know that place has the tightest security in Eerie."

It was true. The people who ran Things went to a lot of trouble to make sure nobody got inside who wasn't supposed to. But I had some inside information I knew would help us.

"My dad took me to his office once," I said. "He told me that there's a back door to the place. They use it when they forget their identification cards and don't want to go through the main doors. I guess the guards there can get pretty touchy if you don't have the right ID."

When we reached the Things, Inc., building, I walked right past the unsmiling guards at the front doors. They didn't even blink as we went by on the sidewalk, although I saw one man's nose wrinkle as he got a whiff of Simon.

As soon as we turned the corner, I ducked into the alley and pulled Simon with me. I went down the trash-filled alley to a big dumpster at the end.

"Ugh," said Simon when we were next to the dumpster. "This smells even worse than we do."

"The door should be right behind here," I said. "Now you know why the guards don't notice it. They wouldn't dare come back here."

I pushed behind the dumpster. Sure enough, there was a door in the wall. I grabbed the handle and pulled, and it came open.

"We're in," I said to Simon, and slipped inside.

We were in a stairwell. The only way to go was up, so I started climbing the stairs.

"Do you know where you're going?" asked Simon.

"Sort of," I answered. "I know my dad works on the fifth floor. I just don't know exactly where."

When we came to the first floor door, I opened it and looked in. All I saw was a long white hallway with rows of doors. They were all shut, and the place was so clean it looked like a hospital.

"Nothing here," I said, and we kept climbing. At each floor I looked in the door, and each one was exactly the same. I didn't see any people. Just hallway after hallway of white tile.

"I don't know exactly what my dad does here," I said to Simon, "but it must be really boring. This place is about as exciting as a trip to the dentist."

When we reached the fifth floor, I opened the door. As I suspected, the hallway was the same as all the others. With Simon following me, I walked to the first door. Painted across the front in black letters it said: PRODUCT TESTING ROOM 51: FOREVERWARE.

"We definitely do not want to go in there," said Simon, shuddering.

We moved on to the next door, which said: PRODUCT TESTING ROOM 52: PIRANHA REPELLENT. Each door we came to listed some other product that was being tested by Things, Inc.: mechanical Christmas tree decorators, edible carpets, cars for pets, or nuclear-powered toasters. But nothing sounded even remotely like vegetables.

Then, at the next to last door, we read: PRODUCT TESTING ROOM 59: EERIE FARMS. But unlike the other doors, this one had an extra message, written in bright red: NO ADMITTANCE: TOP SECRET CLEARANCE REQUIRED.

"This is the place," I said. "This is where my dad has been working for the last couple of weeks."

"Should we just knock?" asked Simon.

I didn't have a better idea, so I rapped three times on the door. There was no answer.

"Dad?" Still no answer.

"Maybe he's at lunch," said Simon.

"Maybe," I said, "but I doubt it."

I went to try the doorknob, but there wasn't one. There was just a slot in the wall next to the door, with a little light over it. The light was flashing red.

"It's an electronic lock," I said. "We need an ID card to get in. This is a dead end."

"Maybe not," said Simon. He was fishing in his back pocket. He pulled something out and held it up.

"What's that?" I asked.

"My library card," he said.

"That won't work," I said. "Don't be ridiculous."

"It's worth a try," said Simon.

He took his card and stuck it into the slot by the door. At first the red light flickered, as though it was thinking about something. Then it suddenly turned green and started blinking.

"Push open the door," said Simon. "Quick, before it changes its mind."

I pushed on the door, and it swung open. Simon pulled his library card out, and we went inside. The door shut behind us with a click.

Inside, the room was dark. I felt around for a light switch, but there wasn't one. There were some lights on the far side of the room, glowing a pale green in the darkness, but they only cast enough light to keep us from bumping into things.

"Why is it so dark?" said Simon.

"I don't know," I said. "What I really want to know is where my dad is."

As my eyes adjusted to the darkness, I was able to make out more of the things in the room. It was a lot larger than I'd first thought, and it was filled with all kinds of equipment that I didn't know the purposes of. Since the only interesting thing seemed to be the glowing green lights, I went toward them.

When I got closer, I realized that the lights were actually in another, smaller room. It was separated from the main room by another door. When I looked through, I saw that someone was standing in the other room with his back to the door. He was standing directly under the lights, which made it look like he was taking a shower in the green light.

"It's my dad!" I said.

I pounded on the glass with my fist, calling out to my dad, but he didn't turn around. "This must be soundproof," I said to Simon. "He can't hear us."

The door separating the rooms did have a handle, and Simon tried it. It opened easily, and I stepped into the room. As soon as I did, I was overwhelmed by the smell of growing plants. The room was very warm, almost like a greenhouse.

"Hey, Dad," I said loudly. "What are you doing in here, trying to grow tropical fruit?"

He still didn't turn around. I ran over to him and tapped him on the back. When he didn't respond, I grabbed his arm and turned him around.

Then I screamed. Because all around my father's face were leaves. Vines wound around his head and hung down his chest. More leaves sprouted from his cuffs, and where his feet were there were roots pushing into the pile of dirt around his shoes. His entire front was covered with tiny yellow blossoms, some of which were turning into little red fruit.

My father had become a tomato plant.

9

I stood there, staring in horror at my father. At least, what used to be my father. He was still there, all right, underneath the vines and the flowers and the ripening tomatoes. I could still see his glasses and his sweater and the watch I'd given him one Christmas on his wrist. But he had turned into something else, too, something I didn't want to look at.

"He's a plant," said Simon simply. "Your dad's a plant."

"This is what they're up to," I said. "They want us all to be turned into vegetables."

All of a sudden, something over our heads clicked on, and a fine mist started to rain down on my father. I jumped out of the way just before the water touched me. Simon and I stood there, watching as the mist settled on the leaves that covered my dad.

"He's being watered," I said. "Just like you'd water a plant. I bet that water has the chemicals in it."

As we looked at my father, his eyes opened. When I saw him looking at me, I screamed. So did Simon.

"Hi there, boys," he said, as though we'd just walked into the kitchen and found him making lunch instead of finding him in a lab turned into a tomato bush.

"Um, hi, Dad," I said.

"Yeah," said Simon. "Hi, Mr. Teller. How are you?"

"Just fine," my dad said. It was weird watching his mouth moving when it was surrounded by leaves. It was like he didn't even notice or anything.

"What are you working on?" I asked him. For some reason, I just couldn't bring myself to ask him how he had been turned into a plant.

He scratched his nose with his hand, sending a tomato falling to the floor, where it landed with a wet splat. "Oh, we're still working on the Eerie Farms project," he said. "It's going very well."

I looked at Simon. I didn't know what to do next. It was clear that my father didn't find anything strange about the fact that there were roots holding him in one spot and that he was almost ready for picking.

"Do you think you'll be coming home soon?" I said finally.

My father laughed. "I'm not sure," he said. "We still have a lot of work to do here."

Before I could ask him any more questions, the mist turned off and the green light was extinguished. As it went out, my dad's eyes closed and he went back to just being a plant.

"Dad?" I said, reaching over and shaking his vine-covered shoulder. He didn't respond.

"What happened to him?" asked Simon. "Why isn't he responding?"

"He thinks it's night," said a voice behind us.

I whirled around to see who was there. A man was standing in the doorway. He was short and a little bit fat. He wore a white lab coat, and his hair was all messed up. In fact, it looked a little bit like a tangle of grass. He had a white glove on one hand.

"You must be Marshall," he said. "Allow me to introduce myself. I am Beauregard Plante."

"Mr. Plante!" I said. "I'm glad you're here. You have to help my dad."

"Help him?" said Mr. Plante. "What do you mean help him? I see nothing wrong with him."

"But he's a plant!" I said. "Look at him."

Mr. Plante walked over to where my dad was standing. He turned to me and smiled. "Not just a plant," he said. "Your father is a perfect specimen of Beauregard's Summer Peach Tomato plant."

"What?" I said. "You mean you know about this?"

He laughed. "Know about it?" he said. "Young man, who do you think began this fantastic experiment?"

"You?" I said weakly as it all became clear to me.

He nodded. "That's right," he said. "You should be very proud of your father. He has become the first success story in my plan."

"What did you mean when you said Mr. Teller thinks it's night?" said Simon.

"Ah, Mr. Holmes," said Mr. Plante. "I see you're a detective, just like your namesake."

"How do you know my name?" said Simon.

"From your library card, of course," he said.

"I knew that was too easy," said Simon, sighing.

"Actually, your smell gave you away," said Mr. Plante. "Someone on the fourth floor complained of a foul odor in the hallways. When we checked the computer system, we found you were in here. Oh, by the way, you should be careful about returning books. I see you're three days overdue on *The UFO Conspiracies*."

"Not to change the subject," I said. "But what have you done to my father?"

"Oh, yes," said Mr. Plante. "As I said, he is sleeping. He thinks it is night because we've turned off the grow lights."

"Okay," I said. "But what have you *done* to him?"

"It's very simple," said Mr. Plante. "He has been treated with a special fertilizer, which has combined the DNA of a tomato plant with your father's own DNA. When the cells in his body divide, the plant DNA is spread throughout his system."

"But why?" I said. "Why would you want to do that?"

"Because," said Mr. Plante, "it's so much more efficient for everyone, don't you see?"

"No," I said. "I don't see."

"Plants are the most extraordinary creatures," said Mr. Plante. "They grow their own food using only sun-

87

light. They produce vegetables that can be eaten. And all they require is a minimum amount of water. But they lack one thing.''

''What's that?'' asked Simon after Mr. Plante had paused for a moment.

''They can't think,'' said Mr. Plante. ''They have no way of communicating. By combining their DNA with that of humans, I can create the perfect living organism, one that requires very little care but is still capable of rational thought.'' He looked at Simon and me triumphantly. ''Besides,'' he said, ''it's a lot of fun, don't you think?''

''I don't think it's fun at all,'' I said. ''I think you're crazy.''

Mr. Plante scowled. ''That's what *they* said, too.''

''They who?'' I said.

''My colleagues,'' he said. ''*They* tried to stop me, too. But they couldn't, and neither can a couple of kids like you.''

''I don't know what you're talking about,'' I said.

''Several years ago, when I first became involved in the field of botany, I was involved in DNA research on plants,'' he said. ''We were attempting to create a line of vegetables that were resistant to drought and pests. One afternoon while attempting an experiment, there was an . . . accident . . . in the lab. I was exposed to a particularly strong sample of plant DNA. Broccoli, to be exact. At first, I thought I was fine. But a few days later, I discovered a green rash on my arm.''

I snuck a glance at Simon. I knew he was also thinking about the rash on his leg and the one on my arm.

"Over the next few weeks, the rash spread," Mr. Plante continued. "I also noticed other changes—intense thirst, a desire to be in the sun for long periods of time. When I began to suspect what was happening, I studied samples of my DNA, and discovered what had happened."

He reached down and pulled the glove off of his hand. Underneath it, where his hand should have been, there was a stalk of broccoli. The five bushy green heads looked like stubby fingers, and the thick stalk went up his sleeve just like an arm would.

"And you didn't try to find a cure?" I said, staring at his broccoli hand.

"Of course not," said Mr. Plante. "This is science! I had discovered something no one had ever seen before. Soon I realized that my accidental discovery could have a greater purpose. But my colleagues thought I was crazy, even when I showed them the proof. They laughed me out of the facility, and I went underground, where I continued to experiment and plan."

"But if you have broccoli DNA in you, why aren't you a plant like my father?" I asked.

"I had to retain my human form long enough to see the experiments through," said Mr. Plante.

"How did you do that?" asked Simon.

"That's not important," said Mr. Plante, waving his hand in the air. "What's important is that I am almost near the end."

89

"And what will that be?" I said.

Mr. Plante grinned. "I have chosen the town of Eerie as the first stop on my way to making the world one big garden," he said. "Soon everyone in Eerie will be treated with the vegetable DNA. As I suspect you know, the Eerie Farms produce contains the super-strong DNA. But that wasn't working fast enough, so I introduced fertilizer into the water supply."

"Yeah, we'd sort of guessed that," said Simon. "As you can tell from our smell."

Mr. Plante ignored him and continued talking. "All it requires now is one final super-strong dose of the DNA fertilizer, and everyone will be blooming."

"How will you do that?" I asked.

He looked at me suspiciously. "Oh, well," he said after a moment. "You won't be going anywhere now, so I might as well tell you. At this weekend's Harvest Days, there will be free samples of our latest product, Eerie Farms vegetable juice. Of course, everyone will want to try it. When they do, the cycle will be completed, and they will begin to sprout."

"But why Eerie?" I said.

"I needed to find someplace very normal," said Mr. Plante. "A place so ordinary that no one would suspect anything until it was too late."

"Boy, have you got the wrong town," said Simon.

"As you know," said Mr. Plante, ignoring him, "Eerie is unremarkable in every way. So I talked my way into a job here at Things, Incorporated, and used their facilities to continue my studies. When Eerie Farms became a client, I saw my chance and took it.''

''But why my dad?''

''When I met your father, I knew he was the perfect man to help me,'' said Mr. Plante. ''He doesn't ask any questions. I hadn't counted on his having a nosy kid.''

''Yeah, well, surprise,'' I said.

''Now that you know,'' said Mr. Plante, ''I'm afraid I can't let you leave here. After all my work, it would be a shame to have it all ruined.''

He reached over and hit a button on the wall with a broccoli finger. The door between the two rooms began to close, locking us in.

''I'll just give you your dose a little earlier than the rest of the town gets theirs,'' he said. ''Since you haven't been bathing, I'll have to make it extra strong.''

He turned to a control panel and began pushing buttons and turning dials. I heard the sprinklers overhead begin to click and whir, and I knew that in a minute the mist that had surrounded my father would be falling down on us, turning us into plants. I had to think of something.

Mr. Plante was just about to hit the button that would spray us with the fertilizer. As he lifted his hand, I charged him. I ran into him as hard as I could, knocking him to the floor. I fell on top of him, and the breath was knocked out of me.

Mr. Plante was struggling, beating his hand and his broccoli stalk against me. He was very strong, and I knew that I couldn't keep him down forever.

"Help me," I called to Simon. "Find something to tie him up with."

I could hear Simon running around the lab, trying to find something. He was pulling things off of shelves and knocking stuff onto the floor. Then I heard him running over to where I was wrestling with Mr. Plante.

"Stand back," said Simon.

I scrambled to my feet and stood away from Mr. Plante as Simon stepped forward. He was holding a spray can.

"What are you doing!" I yelled. "You can't stop him with air freshener or whatever that is."

Simon ignored me. He held down the button on the can. A cloud of spray came out, enveloping Mr. Plante's head in mist. He took a deep breath of it. Then he started coughing, his chest heaving as he tried to breathe. His broccoli stalk hand went to his mouth, covering it as he wheezed.

"Come on," said Simon. "I don't know how long that will hold him off."

Simon hit the button on the wall, and we ran out of the little room. Mr. Plante was still lying on the floor, coughing.

"I'll get you," he tried to shout, but it ended in a coughing fit.

Simon found another button on the other side of the wall and pressed it. The door between the rooms slid down, locking Mr. Plante inside. Simon sprayed the button with the spray can, and it crackled and sparked as it short-circuited.

"That should keep him in there for a while," said Simon.

"What is that stuff?" I asked, pointing at the spray can.

Simon held it up. It was a can of No More Weeds spray.

"They must have been using it in their tests," he said. "I figured that since Mr. Plante is part broccoli, weed killer would probably do something. I just wasn't sure what."

"Good thinking," I said. "Now we just have to get out of here without getting caught."

I looked back into the lab. Mr. Plante had passed out on the floor, but I could see that he was breathing, so I knew he was okay. My father was still asleep in the dark corner. I hated leaving him there like that, but I knew Mr. Plante wouldn't do anything to hurt his prize specimen.

"Don't worry, Dad," I said as Simon and I left the room. "I'll find a way to get you back to normal."

I hoped I was right.

10

*G*etting out of Things, Inc., was a lot easier than I expected. Despite what Mr. Plante had said about the guards knowing we were there, no one was waiting for us in the halls. In fact, we didn't see a single person as we went back down the stairway and out the secret door. Within just a few minutes, we were walking down Main Street again, just as though we were out for a walk and not running away from a crazy scientist who was about to turn all of Eerie into one big vegetable patch.

"Why do you think we got out so easily?" said Simon.

"I think Mr. Plante is being careful," I said. "I don't think he wants anyone at Things to know what he's up to. If he's been doing all of this work in secret, he can't risk being exposed now, not when he's close to the end."

"Which brings us to our next problem," said Simon. "How are we going to stop him?"

The truth was, I didn't have any ideas. I didn't know enough about the science of DNA to know what might work against the fertilizer Mr. Plante was using to change everyone. I didn't even know who to ask. The one person who might know—my dad—was trapped in that laboratory, waiting to be watered and picked.

Simon must have noticed the look on my face. "I'm sorry about your dad," he said.

"That's how we're all going to look if we don't do something," I said. "It's only two days until the Harvest Days festival. If we don't come up with something by then, we'll all be walking tossed salads."

Because we didn't know what else to do, we went back to my house to think. I thought that just maybe I could convince my mother that something weird was happening.

Unfortunately, things didn't work out that way. When Simon and I walked into the kitchen, my mother was sitting at the table. There was a glass in front of her, and it was filled with a brownish liquid. A plastic bottle sat on the table next to her.

"Hi," she said, picking up the glass and taking a big sip. "Want a drink?"

"What is it?" I asked, even though I had a feeling I didn't want to know.

My mother held up the plastic bottle. It was a container of Eerie Farms liquid fertilizer.

"This is just the best," she said. "In fact, your mother is the one who suggested I try it, Simon. She picked some up at the market this afternoon. It's really delicious.''

While my mother hadn't yet started to sprout leaves, her skin was definitely turning green. I guessed that the fertilizer she was drinking was rapidly affecting her system, and that soon she would be looking for a nice place in the garden to settle down.

"Mom, I have something to tell you," I said. "This is going to sound really bizarre, but try to listen to me."

"Sure, Mars," she said, refilling her empty glass. "What's up?"

I took a deep breath. "Well, you remember Dad?"

"Remember him?" said my mom. "Of course I remember him. Why are you talking about him as if he's gone?"

"Well, he sort of is," I said. I didn't know how to tell her that she was now married to a tomato plant.

"What are you talking about, Marshall?" she said. "Is this going to be another one of your stories about UFOs or some such nonsense? I've told you a thousand times—Mayor Chisel is not from outer space, and there are no aliens living in Eerie."

"No, Mom," I said. "This isn't about aliens. At least I don't think it is."

"Then what is it about?" She was looking at me expectantly.

"It's about vegetables," I said.

"Vegetables?"

"Right," I said. "I—um—think that we've been

eating too many of them. I think they're doing things to us."

"The vegetables are doing things to us?" said my mom. "Like what?"

I knew I had to just come out and tell her. Otherwise we'd be there all day. "Dad is a vegetable," I said. "A tomato, actually."

My mother looked at me for a minute. Then she started to laugh. She laughed so hard she started to cry. When she could finally breathe again, she wiped her eyes.

"Oh, Marshall," she said, "that's the funniest thing I've ever heard. Where do you come up with this stuff?"

I looked at Simon helplessly.

"It's true, Mrs. Teller," Simon said. "I saw it. Mr. Teller is a plant. He was exposed to some weird plant DNA or something."

"Now, don't you go encouraging him, Simon," said my mother. "The two of you are just terrible. Next you'll be trying to tell me that *I'm* turning into a vegetable."

I started to try and explain things to her, but I was interrupted by Syndi coming into the kitchen. When I saw her, I knew things were getting way out of control. Her blond hair had turned almost completely green. It looked like she had grass growing out of her head.

"Mom, I need some help," she said. "Look at my hair." She looked really upset, and for a moment I hoped that she had realized what was happening to her.

"What's wrong with it?" my mother asked.

Syndi walked over to the table and bent down. "Just look at it!" she wailed.

I looked at Syndi's hair. It really had turned into some kind of plant tendrils. Now I knew my mother would have to believe what I was saying.

"Oh, my," said my mother as she examined Syndi's hair. "This is terrible."

"See?" I said. "It's happening to Syndi, too. Just like it did to Dad."

"To Dad?" said Syndi. "Dad has aphids?"

"What?" I said, confused.

"Aphids," Syndi said. "I have aphids in my hair."

I looked more closely. Crawling around the tendrils that covered Syndi's head were little green bugs. They were everywhere.

"How am I going to win the Miss Harvest Days contest when I have aphids?" she said, and began to cry.

My mother put her arm around Syndi. "Now, don't cry," she said. "We'll just put some spray on that and your hair will be as good as new."

Syndi kept crying. "But I'm in—in—infested," she sobbed. "None of the other girls will have aph—aph—aphids."

This was too much to take. One of my parents was already a plant. My sister had bugs in her hair. And my mother thought it was all perfectly normal.

"Can't you see what's going on?" I shouted.

My mother and Syndi just stared at me.

"Syndi has *aphids* in her hair," I said to my mother. "And you're drinking *fertilizer*."

"I don't know what's gotten into you, Marshall," my mother said. "But I don't like it at all. You shouldn't be making fun of your sister's problem. This is very serious."

"I know it's serious!" I said. "What do you think I've been trying to tell you? She's turning into a vegetable. You all are."

"Marshall, there's no need to call people names," my mother said. "And there is absolutely no need to be making up crazy stories. Now why don't you go upstairs and lie down? Or maybe take a bath. I don't want to be critical, but you don't smell very pleasant."

There was nothing else I could do. Mr. Plante's fertilizer was obviously working on everyone's brains as well as their bodies. They couldn't tell that something bad was happening.

"Come on," I said to Simon. "Let's go."

"Simon, your mother wants you to come right home," said my mom. "She's making zucchini pie for dinner, and she says it's your favorite."

"Oh, yeah," said Simon. "Zucchini pie. I wouldn't want to miss that." He looked at me and made a face, like he was being sick.

"I guess I'll see you at school tomorrow," I said as he left.

I left my mother and Syndi in the kitchen, picking

the aphids out of her hair, and went to my room. While I had a lot to think about, and important plans to make, the fact was that I was dead tired. After all of the running around Simon and I had done, I could barely keep my eyes open. I laid down on my bed to rest for a minute, and before I knew it I was asleep.

I woke up to my mother knocking on my bedroom door.

"Marshall," she was saying. "Get up. You're going to be late for school."

I rubbed my eyes and dragged myself out of bed. I went to the door and opened it. My mother was standing there in her bathrobe and slippers. Her face was bright green.

"Aaahhh," I said, startled. "You're a plant! I told you it was happening!"

She laughed. Then she rubbed a finger across her cheek. The green came away in a thin streak, and I saw her skin underneath it.

"It's face cream," she said. "Cucumber and avocado. I told you yesterday, I am not a plant."

"Not yet," I said under my breath as she walked down the hallway.

After grabbing my backpack, I went downstairs and snuck out the front door, avoiding the breakfast of fertilizer and beet waffles my mother and Syndi were enjoying in the kitchen. Simon wasn't waiting for me, so I guessed that he'd already gone to school. I only had a few minutes to get there, so I ran. By the time I arrived, I was sweating and smelling worse than ever.

Going to classes that Thursday was one of the oddest things I've ever done. All around me, kids and teachers were in various stages of growth. Some of them had tendrils growing from their heads, while others had leaves and even flowers peeking out from their hair. Almost everyone had greenish skin.

By now I was used to seeing people who looked like walking petunias, but what was even weirder was how nobody even seemed to notice it at all. Miss Earhart stood up in front of the history class with a small eggplant hanging from her chin, and no one said a word. I saw Judy Wilkins walk by, laughing and joking about the movie she'd seen the night before, and nobody even mentioned the ladybugs clinging to her long green curls.

The only thing people thought was weird was me. I smelled so bad that nobody wanted to sit near me in class. As I walked down the hallways, people held their noses and ran the other direction.

"Hey, Teller," said Nick Ricci, who had so much moss on his face it looked like a beard. "What are you trying to do, impersonate a garbage dump?"

"There's that weird kid," said another girl, whose shoes were covered in little vines bursting with purple flowers. "I heard he actually thinks that Bigfoot lives in the Eerie Woods. What a freak."

I ignored them and went to the cafeteria. I looked for Simon, and found him sitting at a table by himself. I went over and sat down. He looked miserable.

"Let me guess," I said. "Everyone says you stink."

"You got it," he said. "Everywhere I go, people tell me I'm worse than a skunk or a pair of dirty sweat socks."

"Just be glad all you do is smell," I said. "It could be a lot worse. They just don't realize it."

"Have you thought of anything to do yet?" he asked. I shook my head. "No."

"Do you think Mr. Plante has gotten out by now?"

"Probably," I said. "He might even have men out looking for us."

Simon sighed. "This just gets worse and worse," he said. "What could possibly happen next?"

Just then, something hit me in the back of the head. It was a piece of broccoli. I turned around to see who had thrown it. At the table behind me, Jesse Gingrich and his friends were all laughing.

"Hey, stinky," Jesse yelled. "Why don't you and your buddy head on over to the zoo? I hear they need someone to make the smell in the monkey house even worse."

"Just ignore him," I said to Simon.

Someone tossed a bean at us, and it hit Simon's arm.

"I've seen less dirt in a barnyard," said Rosemary Plotz, and everyone started to laugh.

"Yeah," said someone I couldn't see. "Why don't you guys take a shower?"

Simon stood up. His face was bright red. I could tell he was about to say something that was going to get us into trouble, but it was too late. I couldn't stop him.

"Why don't you make us?" he shouted. "You stupid plant-heads!"

There was a moment of silence. Then someone began chanting, "Show—er. Show—er. Show—er."

Some other kids joined in, and soon the entire cafeteria was filled with the sounds of people shouting, "Show—er. Show—er. Show—er."

Simon looked at me. "Uh-oh," he said.

But it was already too late. Before I knew it, someone had picked me up and hoisted me into the air. I was being held up by a lot of hands. I looked over and saw that Simon, too, had been picked up. Then everyone started moving out of the cafeteria.

"Put us down!" I yelled. I tried to thrash around, but there were too many people holding me.

"Show—er! Show—er! Show—er!" chanted the kids as they carried Simon and I down the hallway toward the boys' gym. I looked everywhere for someone to help us, but there were no teachers around. I had a terrible feeling they were all watching from behind closed doors, laughing as Simon and I were taken away.

The mob of kids stormed into the boys' locker room and went to the showers. Jesse Gingrich, who had started it all, went over and turned the knobs on the wall, sending water spraying into the room.

"Throw them in!" he yelled.

I knew that the water was filled with the chemicals Mr. Plante had been dumping into the water. If Simon and I were covered in it, we'd be in big trouble. I began to kick and scream, trying to get away. From the sounds around me, I knew Simon was doing the same thing.

I had almost gotten away from the hands holding me when someone gave me a big push. My feet slipped, and I skidded across the shower floor toward the water. I tried to regain my balance, but then someone shoved Simon, and we collided. Both of us went sliding backwards.

I felt the first drops of water hit my skin. Then I was right under the spray. As the water covered me and Simon, the crowd of kids erupted in a giant cheer.

We were soaked right through. Although I got up and turned the water off, it was too late. Both Simon and I had been completely drenched by the shower.

"Now we'll start turning into plants, too," said Simon. "Won't we?"

"I think so," I said. "We'll have to wait and see."

After everything we'd done to avoid coming into any further contact with the chemicals, now we were dripping with the stuff. Our clothes were sopping wet. As we shuffled out of the shower, the kids all pointed at us and laughed.

"Hey, you sure smell a lot better now," snickered Jesse.

I ignored him and the rest of the kids. I walked out of the locker room with Simon, leaving a wet trail behind us. I could practically feel the fertilizer soaking into me, and I wondered if the plant DNA was already mixing with my own.

Since there was nothing else we could do, Simon and I left the school. Once we were out in the sun, we started to dry a little, but we were still miserable. Even worse, the sunlight seemed to be making the fertilizer work even faster. We hadn't walked a block before the rash on my arm started to itch. I looked at the green patch. Right before my eyes, it began to spread out.

"Oh, great," I said. "It's starting already."

Simon rolled up his pants and looked at the rash on his leg. It, too, was growing, slowly but steadily.

"How long do you think it will take?" he asked.

"Probably a day or two," I said.

"That doesn't give us much time," said Simon.

"It won't really matter," I said. "The Harvest Days festival starts tomorrow, and that's when Mr. Plante plans on giving everyone the last dose to turn them all into vegetables."

"I just hope I don't turn into an onion," said Simon. "I really hate onions."

"We have to get out of the light," I said. "I think darkness slows the chemicals down. At least that will give us some time to think of something."

We began to walk to my house, moving quickly so that we could get there as soon as possible. My sneakers made wet squelching sounds on the sidewalk as I moved. I couldn't wait to get home and change into dry clothes.

We turned the corner by World of Stuff and almost walked right into a giant ear of corn. It was being carried by two men, who set it up on the sidewalk. The whole street was lined with giant vegetables. But they weren't real. They were plastic. I found that out when I went over and tapped on one of the big stalks of asparagus.

"What is all this?" said Simon.

"They must be getting ready for the weekend," I said.

As it turned out, that's exactly what was happening. All up and down Main Street, workers were setting up giant vegetables or hanging banners from the streetlights. Big yellow flags covered with pictures of tomatoes and lettuce and peppers fluttered everywhere, and there were signs all over the walls saying, EERIE PRODUCE—SO GOOD, IT'S UNNATURAL!

"I wonder if these guys know what they're setting up for," Simon said.

"Probably not," I said. "They're probably just like everyone else in town. They just think it's a big picnic."

We had to walk through the crowd of Eerie Farms employees in order to get home. I tried not to look at any of them as we passed, in case Mr. Plante had warned them about us or anything. But they were so busy carrying the vegetables and hanging signs that they didn't even notice us.

It wasn't until we were almost about to turn off of the street when I saw Mr. Plante walking toward us. He was carrying a clipboard, and he was talking loudly to Bud, who was nodding in agreement.

"We have to have the broccoli forest set up over there," Mr. Plante was saying. "That way when the people come out they'll be headed right for . . ."

He looked up and saw us. Our eyes locked, and I saw him frown. Then he yelled. "Get them!" he shouted. "Get those kids!"

Before we could even start to run, two Eerie Farms hands had grabbed us and were holding us tight. It was the second time in the last hour that I'd been caught, and I wasn't liking it.

"Let go of us!" I screamed. "Do you know what this man is doing? He's trying to turn everyone in Eerie into . . ."

A hand clamped shut over my mouth. It was Mr. Plante's. He leaned down and whispered in my ear, "Keep quiet, or I'll make sure your father is turned into tomato sauce. Do you understand?"

I looked into his eyes. I could see that he wasn't kidding. I slowly nodded my head.

"Good," he said. "Now you and your friend are going to take a little ride with me. I'm going to make sure you're out of the way during tomorrow's festivities."

He motioned for the two men to take us over to a waiting car. They opened the back door and pushed us in. Then Mr. Plante and Bud got into the front. The car took off, driving out of town.

Nobody said a word during the drive. Simon and I both knew it wouldn't do any good, so we just kept quiet. When the car finally pulled to a stop outside the barn at Eerie Farms, Bud opened the door and we got out.

"Bring them in here," said Mr. Plante.

Bud shoved us roughly toward the barn doors. Mr. Plante opened them, and we went inside. It looked just as it had the day Simon and I had broken in. Mr. Plante walked through the room and over to the door marked DECONTAMINATION AREA. He punched a sequence of numbers into a control pad next to the door, and it opened with a soft whooshing sound.

Mr. Plante, Bud, Simon, and I walked through the door, and Mr. Plante punched in another code so that the doors shut. We were in a large room. One wall was lined with what looked like tall boxes with round glass windows in them. The rest of the room was filled with tables covered with various kinds of scientific equipment.

"What are you going to do to us?" I asked.

Mr. Plante smiled. "Don't worry," he said. "This won't hurt you a bit. I'm just going to make it a little easier to keep an eye on you."

"How are you planning on doing that?" asked Simon.

"Step over here," said Mr. Plante.

He walked over to one of the tall boxes and opened the door. Bud pushed us over to it.

"What is that?" I asked.

"Why don't I show you?" he said. He grabbed Simon's shoulder and shoved him into the box. Before Simon could even turn around, Mr. Plante had shut and locked the door. All I could see was Simon's face pressed against the glass as he beat on the door.

Mr. Plante pushed a button on the box and Simon lit up with green light, just like the light my dad had been bathed in back at Things, Inc. Suddenly, I knew what was going to happen. So did Simon, because he started pounding on the door furiously.

Mr. Plante just laughed and turned a control knob on the box. The familiar mist began to fall all around Simon. It fell so heavily that soon I couldn't even see his face through it. All I could see was his shadow moving around. And as I watched, strange forms began to move around, too—long, thin fingers that seemed to be wrapping around him.

Mr. Plante turned off the mist. As it cleared, I saw what had happened to Simon. He'd been turned into a plant. In fact, he had been turned into a string bean plant. His whole body was covered in green leaves, and from various points on the vines, fully formed beans were hanging. His eyes were still open, and he was looking at himself in horror. Then he looked right at me.

"At least you're not an onion," I mouthed to him.

"Now it's your turn," said Mr. Plante.

Bud held me firmly by the shoulder and pushed me into the box next to Simon's. I didn't even try to fight. I knew it would be pointless, and I'd just end up in even more trouble, if that was possible.

Before he closed the door to my box, Mr. Plante said, "I'll be back for you after tomorrow's little festivities. By then, it will be too late for you to cause any trouble."

"We'll just see about that," I said, unable to resist myself.

The door shut, and Mr. Plante turned on the green light. Then he hit the button, and I felt the mist raining over me. I felt my skin begin to tingle. Then things began to grow around me. It didn't hurt at all; it felt almost like being tickled. A vine crept across my forehead, and I felt leaves growing around my neck.

Then it was all over. The mist was turned off, and the box started to clear. When I could see, I looked down at myself and saw that I'd become a squash. Big leaves fanned out from my body, and several yellow squashes hung from my vines. I could feel my hands and my feet, but they seemed to be rooted in place. All I could do was move my head around.

Mr. Plante grinned at me through the window of the box. Then he turned around, and I saw him and Bud leave the room. The door clicked shut, and Simon and I were left alone.

For a couple of hours, all I could do was watch myself grow. It was weird seeing the blossoms ripen into vegetables. It was hard to believe that it was really my body that had merged with the plant. But I couldn't deny what was happening. I wondered if Simon was feeling the same things I was.

Then, suddenly, the light above me shut off, plunging me into darkness. My eyes started to grow heavy, and I couldn't keep them open. As I fell asleep, my last thought was that the boxes must have been on automatic lighting and watering timers.

While I slept, I dreamed about being a plant. In my dream, I was planted in a garden. My mother, father, and Syndi were all there too. Syndi was an eggplant. My mother was a stalk of corn, and my father was still a tomato. We were all sitting in the sun, soaking up the rays. I felt happy.

Then Mr. Plante came along. He was dressed as a farmer, and he had a big basket with him. He walked into our garden and stopped in front of me.

"It's time for harvest," he said.

I didn't want him to pick me or my family. I tried to say something, but I couldn't. I tried to run away, but my roots were stuck firmly in the ground. Mr. Plante just started to laugh at me. Then I saw his big hand coming toward me, and I tried to scream. But all that happened was that my leaves began to tremble.

"Wake up," said a voice just as Mr. Plante's hand closed around one of my squashes.

I opened my eyes. The door to my box was open, and there was a man looking in at me. It was Pete, the worker I'd seen get covered with the pumpkin juice.

"Don't say anything," Pete said to me.

He held up a spray bottle and pointed it at me. I was afraid it was some kind of poison. Pete squeezed the trigger, and I was covered in a cloud of spray. I closed my eyes, waiting to wilt.

Instead, I started to change. The leaves and vines that surrounded my body withered and fell to the floor. The squashes tumbled out of the box. I looked down at my skin and saw that it was no longer green. It was its normal pink color.

"What is that stuff?" I asked Pete.

"It's an antidote to the fertilizer," he said. "It counteracts the effects of the plant DNA."

"Thanks," I said. "But why did you help me?"

"I know what it's like to be a plant," he said.

"I saw you that day," I told him. "I wondered what happened to you."

"Mr. Plante used me for experiments," he said. "He brought me in here. But instead of decontaminating me, he let me turn into a pumpkin plant."

"How'd you get back to normal?"

"He needed someone to try the antidote on," Pete explained. "He used me. When I got back to normal, I pretended to forget all about ever having been a plant. So he left me alone."

"But you didn't forget," I said.

Pete shook his head. "No," he said. "I remembered the dreams."

"About being in the garden?" I said.

"Yes. I think that must be what all plants dream about—getting picked," said Pete.

I shuddered. "I'm glad that's over."

I stepped out of the box. Then we opened Simon's box and returned him to normal.

"Man, am I glad to be rid of those leaves," said Simon. "I had one right under my nose, and I kept sneezing. How long were we in those boxes, anyway?"

"I found you this morning when I came to work," said Pete. "You must have been in there all night."

"Pete," I said, "is there any more of that antidote?"

"There's one barrel of it," he said. "That's all Mr. Plante made. He uses it to keep himself from turning all the way into a plant, or in case something unexpected happens."

"Well, something unexpected *is* about to happen," I said.

Pete and Simon looked at me. "What are you thinking of?" Pete said.

I smiled. "Let's get that barrel," I said. "We're going to crash a party."

12

The Harvest Days festival was scheduled to begin at noon, and it was already ten o'clock. That didn't give us much time to get ready. I explained my plan to Simon and Pete, and then we got going.

Almost everyone who worked at Eerie Farms was working at the festival, so it was easy for us to get the barrel of antidote and load it onto a truck. When we reached Eerie, I had Pete drop Simon and me off at my house. Then he went into town with the antidote to wait for us.

My house was empty when we went in, which was just how I wanted it. Simon and I ran upstairs and went into Syndi's room.

"Are you sure this is going to work?" said Simon.

"No," I said. "I'm not sure at all. But it's the only idea I have, so we have to go with it."

I opened Syndi's closet and looked through her dresses. I picked one covered with blue and yellow flowers and pulled it out. Then I saw another one, a short red one, and took that, too.

"Okay," I said, handing the red one to Simon. "That should fit you. This one is mine."

Simon looked at the dress. "I can't believe we're doing this," he said.

"Just put it on," I told him.

He pulled the dress over his head. It was a little big, but it looked okay. I put the flowered one on.

"Zip me up," I said to Simon, turning around.

He zipped the dress closed, and I looked at myself in the mirror. I looked ridiculous.

"Maybe it will look better when I put the wig on," I said.

I went into the spare bedroom and opened the closet. Inside was a big box of Halloween costumes that my mother had saved over the years. I opened it up and rummaged around until I found the wigs that my mother and Syndi wore the year they had gone trick-or-treating as mermaids. The hair on the wigs was made out of fake blue and green seaweed, and it looked just like vines.

I put one of the wigs on Simon and then put the other one on my head. We straightened the hair, and the wigs actually looked like we had some kind of plants on our heads. Once I stuck some plastic flowers in them, it looked even better.

I found a tube of green face makeup in the box and squeezed some onto my hand. I rubbed it all over my face and arms until it looked like I was covered with the green plant rash everyone in Eerie had. Simon did the same thing.

"Well, that's as good as it's going to get," I said when we were finished.

"Do you really think we'll fool anyone in the Miss Harvest Days contest?" Simon asked.

"If they don't get too close, we might," I said. "Besides, there's no time to worry about that now. We have to go."

We ran out of the house and down the street. Having never had a dress on before, I didn't know how to run in it, and I kept tripping. But eventually I got the hang of it, and before long we were in downtown Eerie.

The Harvest Days festival was in full swing when we arrived. All up and down the street, guys from Eerie Farms were handing out samples of various vegetables. There were fried beets and corn-on-a-stick, pumpkin pies and spinach yogurt. Everywhere we looked, there were people eating the produce.

But the biggest spectacle was in front of the town hall. On the lawn, right next to the statue of Zebediah Eerie, a big stage had been set up. A brass band was playing the Eerie Farms jingle over and over, and there were balloons and streamers everywhere. Off to one side of the stage was a big object covered by a sheet.

"That must be the tank of vegetable juice," I said to Simon. "I bet they're going to unveil it right after the Miss Harvest Days contest."

"I sure hope Pete was able to get here," said Simon. "If he didn't, we're sunk."

"Just keep your fingers crossed," I said.

We walked over to the Town Hall and went up to the table where contestants for Miss Harvest Days were registering. Two women sat behind the table.

"Hi," I said, trying to disguise my voice so I sounded like a girl. "My friend and I would like to enter the contest."

The women smiled. "Why, of course," one of them said. "Just fill out these applications. The contest will begin in about fifteen minutes."

Simon and I sat down on a bench and filled out the applications.

"What names should we use?" Simon asked.

"You be Jasmine Daniels," I said. "I'll be Lily Desmond."

"Where'd you come up with those?" said Simon.

"I don't know," I said. "They just sound pretty."

We wrote down our new names and filled out the rest of the questionnaire. There were a lot of questions, and it took a while.

"What hobbies do I have?" Simon asked. "I mean, does Jasmine have."

"I don't know," I said. "Just put down anything."

We finished the forms and handed them in. As we were leaving, I saw Syndi and my mother approaching the table. I turned my head so they wouldn't see my face and walked right by them. Out of the corner of my eye, I saw Syndi turn and look.

"That girl has on the same dress I bought just last

week," she said. "The saleswoman told me I was the only one in Eerie with that dress."

Luckily for me, she had to fill out her forms, too, so I was able to get away before she said anything else. Simon and I stood next to the stage and waited for the pageant to begin. When the brass band stopped playing, we knew it was time.

Mr. Plante walked out of the crowd and onto the stage. He went to the microphone and tapped it. A horrible screeching sound filled the air.

"Is this thing on?" he said, and everyone laughed.

"Ladies and gentlemen," he said. "It is my pleasure to welcome you to the Eerie Farms Harvest Days. As you know, this is a celebration to mark the introduction of a brand new Eerie Farms product."

The audience erupted in applause. Mr. Plante motioned for them to be quiet.

"I know you're all very excited," he said. "But before we reveal our newest addition to the Eerie Farms line, we're going to crown our Miss Harvest Days. The lucky girl chosen will get to be the first one to sample the new taste sensation we have in store for you."

The audience went wild, clapping and cheering. When they settled down, Mr. Plante continued.

"Let's have all of the contestants up onstage," he said.

Simon and I went up the stairs with the other contestants, trying to blend in. There were seven of us in all, and Simon and I were the last ones in line. We all lined up across the back of the stage.

"Aren't they lovely?" said Mr. Plante, and the audience cheered. I was so nervous I was sweating like crazy. I hoped the makeup wasn't running down my face.

"I think I'm going to throw up," Simon whispered.

"Just keep smiling," I said.

"Since all of our contestants today are equally beautiful," Mr. Plante said, "we're going to choose our Miss Harvest by asking each girl a question. Contestant number one, will you please come forward?"

The first girl walked over to the microphone and stood next to Mr. Plante.

"What is your name?" Mr. Plante asked.

"Amber Buttons," said the girl.

"It says here that your hobbies are painting, playing the tuba, and gardening," said Mr. Plante.

"That's right," said Amber. "I just love to garden."

"Well, then," said Mr. Plante, "here's your question. Why do you think vegetables are important?"

"I think vegetables are important because they add so much to our lives," said Amber. "They're good for us and make us strong."

When she was done, the audience clapped.

"What a wonderful answer," said Mr. Plante. "Now let's hear from our next contestant."

The next contestant was Syndi. She walked over to the microphone and waved to the audience. I had to admit, she looked great, even if she did have aphids.

"This is Syndi Teller," said Mr. Plante, reading the

card in his hand. "Her hobbies are swimming, reading, and nuclear science."

"Nuclear science?" I said to Simon. "She can't even use the microwave."

Syndi had the same question as Amber. She looked out at the audience, took a deep breath, and said, "I think vegetables are important because they bring us all closer together. When we love vegetables, we can't help but love each other, too."

The audience loved her answer. They jumped up, cheering and calling out Syndi's name.

"Well, I guess we have a favorite already," said Mr. Plante. "This is going to be a tough contest."

I stood listening to each of the contestants as they gave their answers to Mr. Plante's question. Finally, it was Simon's turn. He walked shakily over to the microphone and stood there staring at the audience. I could tell he was terrified.

"Our next contestant is the lovely Jasmine Daniels," said Mr. Plante. "It says here her hobbies are stargazing, collecting comic books, and looking for Bigfoot."

There was a pause after Mr. Plante read that, as everyone looked at Simon.

"Well, those are certainly interesting hobbies for a young lady," said Mr. Plante. "Now, why don't you tell everyone why you think vegetables are important?"

"Well," said Simon, "I guess vegetables are important because my mom says I have to eat them or I can't watch TV."

There was dead silence from the audience as everyone just stared at Simon. Mr. Plante had a pained look on his face. He tried to laugh.

"That's a very funny answer, Jasmine," he said. "You're a real kidder."

Simon turned around and came back to the line.

"What was that all about?" I said.

"I just blanked," he said. "I couldn't think of anything so I said whatever came out."

We didn't have time to talk because Mr. Plante was calling me to the microphone.

"Now for our last contestant," he said. "Miss Lily Desmond."

"Hello," I said shyly.

"Lily, it says here that you like to write poetry, play croquet, and help others."

"Why yes," I said. I'd picked those hobbies because the Miss America contestants always said things like that.

Mr. Plante smiled. "Audience, would you like to hear one of Lily's poems?"

The audience cheered. Mr. Plante looked at me. I panicked. I had no idea what to say. I wished that I'd put down something like stamp collecting instead. But they were all waiting for me to say something.

I cleared my throat and leaned into the microphone.

"Apples are red," I said. "Oranges are sweet, lemons are yellow, and peaches are neat. But none are as healthy and nothing can beat—the taste of a freshly picked Eerie Farms beet."

When I finished, the audience went wild. They were yelling out my fake name, waving their hands in the air and calling out, "Encore! Encore!"

The audience kept cheering even when I went back to the line of contestants. Mr. Plante went over to the panel of judges and they handed him a piece of paper. He went back to the microphone and motioned for everyone to settle down.

"All right," he said. "I have the results of our contest in my hand, and it's time to announce the winner. Third place goes to Amber Buttons."

Amber went forward and Mr. Plante handed her a trophy, a stalk of celery dipped in bronze.

"Second place goes to Syndi Teller," he said next.

Syndi's prize was a silver asparagus stalk. She stood beside Amber, looking unhappy. I knew she was mad about not winning.

"And first place—the title of Miss Harvest Days—goes to Lily Desmond!"

The crowd stood up, applauding and cheering as I went forward. Mr. Plante handed me a gold-covered ear of corn. He also placed a tiara on my head.

"And now for the moment we've all been waiting for," he said. "Our new Miss Harvest Days will unveil the newest delicious Eerie Farms product."

Mr. Plante led me over to the side of the stage and handed me the end of a rope. "If you would just pull this, Lily," he said.

I tugged on the rope, and the sheet fell off of the

thing at the side of the stage. It was a giant tub filled with vegetable juice. The vegetable juice that contained enough fertilizer to turn everyone in Eerie into plants.

The audience oohed and aahed over the juice as Mr. Plante talked.

"Before we give out free samples to all of you," he said, "the first taste of Eerie Farms Unnaturally Good Vegetable Juice goes to Miss Harvest Days. Lily, if you would do the honors."

He handed me a ladle. I looked at it, then at the big vat of juice.

"Could you pour me some?" I asked sweetly.

Mr. Plante smiled. "Of course I can," he said.

I handed Mr. Plante the ladle and he leaned over to scoop me up some juice. When he was leaning far enough out over the open tub, I gave him a push with all my strength. For a moment he swayed at the edge of the stage, balancing himself. Then I gave him an extra poke with my corn cob trophy, and over he went. He landed in the vegetable juice with a gigantic splash.

"What have you done?" he screamed as he bobbed in the juice. "I can't swim."

He went under. When he came back up, I saw that he had started to turn green, and I knew that the fertilizer was working. He went under again. This time when he came up, there were leaves all over his body. When he waved his hands around, I saw that there were little buds on the fingers of his good hand. He looked at me, and I pulled off my wig.

"You!" he shouted.

"I told you not to underestimate me," I said as he went under for the third time.

When he came up for the last time, Mr. Plante was nothing but one giant broccoli plant. There was nothing left of the man he had been. The super-strength DNA in the vegetable juice had done its job, and he was finished.

Pete came running up to the stage. "You did it," he said. "You really did it."

I looked out at the audience. Everyone was staring up at me with horrified expressions on their faces.

"We did it, all right," I said to Pete. "But we're still not finished."

EPILOGUE

While I calmed the audience down, Pete wheeled out the barrel of antidote, and we gave everybody a dose of it. It worked almost instantly, and within an hour everybody was back to normal. But as the leaves and fruit and vines disappeared, so did the memories of what had happened.

"What are we doing out here?" said my mother when she was back to her normal self again.

"It's a long story," I said. "We'll talk about it later."

The next thing we did was gather up all of the Eerie Farms produce and load it into a truck.

"I'll take it all back to the farm and destroy it," said Pete. "I'll also dust the crops that are left with antidote so they'll be safe to eat."

"It wouldn't hurt to pour some of that into Lake Eerie, either," I said. "Just in case."

"What about him?" Simon said, pointing to Mr. Plante. His broccoli body was still floating in the tub of vegetable juice.

"Don't worry," said Pete. "We'll put him some-where where he can't cause any trouble. There's a nice sunny spot by the barn that has some good soil."

Pete got some men to help him load the tub of juice and Mr. Plante into a truck. Then he got in and waved good-bye to us.

"Can we go home now?" said Simon. "I'm dying to get out of this dress."

"You go on," I said. "I have one last thing to do. But I need your library card for it."

Simon gave me his card, and I ran all the way to Things, Inc. I slipped in the back door and ran up the stairs to my dad's office. The lock had been repaired so I used Simon's card to go in. Dad was still standing in the lab, covered in leaves. I went in and took a bottle out of my pocket. I'd saved some of the antidote.

I sprinkled the antidote over my dad's head and waited. At first, nothing happened, and I was afraid that he'd been a plant for too long to return to normal. But then the leaves on his arms started to shrink, and soon the vines fell off as well. When it was all over, my dad was standing there in his sweater and pants, looking like he always did.

"Mars!" he said when he turned around and saw me. "What are you doing here?"

"Just stopped by for a visit," I said.

"It's good to see you," my dad said. "But I have a lot of work to do. We're getting ready for the big Eerie Farms campaign, you know."

"Actually," I said, "I just ran into Mr. Plante outside. He says to tell you that the account has been canceled, and to go home."

My dad frowned. "Really?" he said. "That's too bad. We were having a lot of fun."

"I'm sure something better will come up," I said.

"I guess you're right," he said. "Come to think of it, I'm a little tired. I guess I've been in here too long."

He got his coat from the other room, and we started to leave. As we walked out the door, he pulled something from his pocket. It was a tomato.

"I wonder how that got there?" he said. "I don't even like tomatoes."

I took it from him and put it in my pocket. This was going right into the Evidence Locker. "It was probably a sample you were using or something."

"That's probably it," he said. "But Mars?"

"Yes, Dad?"

"Why are you wearing a dress?"

Rubidoux

Two days ago. That's when it all started. I was sitting in class. Planetoid Roma, Diplomatic Universal Headquarters. We call it "DUH." I don't mean to brag, but DUH is where all the smartest life forms in the universe are sent to become intergalactic diplomats.

Like most of the other kids, I've been at school on this chunk of rock since I was five. Scary, huh? Actually it's not all that bad. Being sent to DUH is the highest honor there is. There are 127 worlds in the Planetary Union. And it's the diplomats who hold it all together.

So what do we do at DUH? Study, study, study.

Bor-r-ring! Especially this class: Dead and Dying Worlds 101. If they are dead—over, gone, *done for*—why worry about them? The places I want to know about are the war-torn, hostile places. That's where all the cool stuff happens. You see, the Planetary Union, or PU, is worried about violence from these worlds spreading to us and infecting our peace. So the Union sends secret missions to these planets.

The top mission specialists get to mingle with the locals. They teach them about peace, then get out. If the planet eventually gets it, they are asked to join the Union. If peace is too hard a concept to wrap their minds around, we cut them off—forever. Now that's my idea of a cool job!

I was daydreaming about being on a mission to one of these planets, when suddenly I heard . . . "Roma to Rubidoux. Hello! Professor Toesis here. We're waiting for your answer."

Panicked, I came up with the only response that made sense. "Huh?"

"No, DUH, Mr. Doux. Remember? You're in class studying to become a guardian of our culture. A diplomat of peace. The hope of the Union. With your attention span I fear for the future, Mr. Doux."

"No, no, I'm with you."

"Then would you care to explain the meaning of the golden arches?"

Ugh! Not Earth again. Who cares about the least known of the lesser planets?

Glaring at me, the professor cleared his many throats. I stood up. But nothing came. Not one thought. I was breathing hard. My palms were sweating. Then, just as the professor started stomping down the aisle toward me—one breath from the sulfur-sucking Professor Hal E. Toesis and you are dead meat—a tentacle on my left lower lobe began to jiggle. Hallelujah! Saved!

"The golden arches were found on religious temples scattered all over Earth," I said, stopping Toesis in his tracks. "People would visit them three times a day to feed their souls by inhaling a thin, brown, rubbery disc covered by a red, sweet, sticky substance on a sesame seed bun."

"Very good, Mr. Doux. Perhaps there's hope for the Union yet. You may sit down."

I took my seat next to my best friend, Xela (she pronounces it Shay-la). She's the only thing that makes this very dead class bearable. Leaning over she whispered, "Pulled that one off by the skin of your tentacle."

I wiggled my antennae at her. "Thanks to you."

"You should be thanking the six stars of Erin you can read minds," Xela said with a laugh.

It's true that, like everyone from Douxwhop, I'm telepathic. Well . . . sometimes. At fourteen, I've got a long way to go before I'm great at it. But with Toesis breathing down my neck, I'll take what I can get. Or what thoughts Xela's willing to send me.

"Actually, Xela, I'm going to thank them for making you a genius. So I don't have to be." That's one of the things I like about Xela. She's smart. Really smart. One look into her huge yellow pupils and you know there's more than air filling the space between her lobes. But she doesn't brag about it. She's cool.

Which is more than you can say about some of the life forms around here. Take the guy sitting in front of me. At least I think he's sitting. His name is She-Rak. And he looks like a tadpole with spiked hair. When he eats he chews up his food, then smears it on his skin so he can soak up the nutrients. Trust me, he's no one to take on a picnic.

Then there's Gogol. He's the weirdest specimen of all. Smooth skin. Straight hair. No scales. No antennae. I know not everyone in the universe can have the good looks of Douxwhopians—tall, bronze leathery skin, masses of braided, purple tentacles—but this is one sick-looking puppy.

Just look at him, I thought. *Hand's in the air. As always. Probably can't wait to correct something I said. And check out old Hal E. Toesis. He beams whenever Gogol speaks up.*

"Yes, Gogol?"

"To add a little something about the golden arches . . ."

Blah, blah, blah. I just had to tune him out. It was a matter of survival.

"Who let him into this school anyway?" I whispered to Xela.

"Come on, have a heart."

"No, thanks, I already have four."

"Very funny, Rubi. If you ask me, Gogol's not that bad. In fact, I kind of like him."

"Like him? He looks weird. He acts weird. He *is* weird."

"I don't know. I think he's kind of cute."

All at once, the professor's voice boomed, "Excuse me, are we interrupting you two?"

I gave him my most winning smile. "Not at all, Professor Toesis. We were just discussing . . . life forms. Earthling life forms . . . that's it, isn't it Xela?"

"Care to share your findings with the class?" asked the professor.

"Yes, Xela, care to share our findings?" I was hoping she'd come up with something. Anything. And she did.

"You owe me one," Xela whispered as she rose from her seat. "Professor Toesis, since Gogol seems to be the expert on dead worlds, perhaps he'd like to tell us what he knows."

A look of pure joy spread across Gogol's face. This guy was so sickening he made eating with She-Rak sound good. Naturally, he jumped up.

"While no actual pictures exist of what Earthlings looked like, our scientists believe that they took a variety of forms. Some walked upright on two feet. Some were furry and walked on four feet. Some flew."

"Excellent, Mr. Gogol. And now, Mr. Doux."

Thankfully, the hitsu chimed just in time. "Got to go, Professor Toesis. Can't be late for my next class." I vaulted over the furniture and grabbed Xela's arm as she headed for the door. "Xela, meet me after dinner at the usual place."

"I don't know, Rubi. All day long I've had this really bad feeling. Maybe we shouldn't . . ."

"Don't tell me you're scared!"

"I didn't say that."

"You don't need to," I said, wiggling my antennae.

"Rubi, do me a favor and put a hat on it."

I stared hard. Right into Xela's yellow eyes. "And you, do me a favor. Be there."

EERIE INDIANA is the center of weirdness for the entire planet, the number one landing site for UFOs in the country... But for some strange reason, only 13-year-old Marshall Teller and his 10-year-old friend Simon Holmes notice it!

Watch the #1 hit television series every week!

© 1997 Fox Kids

THINGS CAN'T GET ANY EERIER
... OR CAN THEY?

Don't miss a single book!

#1: Return to Foreverware   by Mike Ford
79774-7/$.99 US/$.99 Can

#2: Bureau of Lost   by John Peel
79775-5/$3.99 US/$4.99 Can

#3: The Eerie Triangle   by Mike Ford
79776-3/$3.99 US/$4.99 Can

#4: Simon and Marshall's
Excellent Adventure   by John Peel
79777-1/$3.99 US/$4.99 Can

#5: Have Yourself
an Eerie Little Christmas   by Mike Ford
79781-X/$3.99 US/$4.99 Can

#6: Fountain of Weird   by Sherry Shahan
79782-8/$3.99 US/$4.99 Can

#7: Attack of the
Two-Ton Tomatoes   by Mike Ford
79783-6/$3.99 US/$4.99 Can

IF YOU DARE TO BE SCARED...
READ SPINETINGLERS!
by M.T. COFFIN